Neverland's Key: A Pirate Princess's Last Chance

The Pirate Princess Chronicles, Volume 3

R.V. Bowman

D1531032

Published by R.V. Bowman, 2019.

NEVERLAND'S KEY: A PIRATE PRINCESS'S LAST CHANCE

First edition. October 23, 2019.

Written by R.V. Bowman.

Also by R.V. Bowman

The Pirate Princess Chronicles
Hook's Daughter: The Untold Tale of a Pirate Princess
Pan's Secret: A Pirate Princess's Quest for Answers
Neverland's Key: A Pirate Princess's Last Chance

Watch for more at www.rvbowman.com.

In Loving Memory of My Grandmother,

Vera Wakonen Craig

(October 18, 1918 - February 2, 1998),

Who introduced me to some of my favorite authors

and regularly fed my love of books.

Chapter 1:
Problems Already

"What do you think, Rommy?"

Finn's voice startled Rommy from the mesmerizing shadows the fire cast on the fabric walls of Little Owl's curiously round home. She looked over at Finn.

He was sitting crossed-legged on the floor on the other side of the fire. He leaned against the rocking chair where Little Owl sat. The older woman had her arm around Alice. The little girl was still distraught over Lobo's death, and although her tears had dried, she leaned against Little Owl.

Rommy swallowed and blinked back tears of her own. The big black wolf had saved her life and lost his own. Without Lobo, it was unlikely they would have ever gotten the answers they needed to seal Peter Pan in Neverland forever.

And now Pan had Francie, too.

Worry made a tight band in Rommy's chest and the question of whether it was all worth it gnawed at the back of her mind. She shook it away. They had to stop Pan from stealing children, and this wasn't the time for tears or questions. They didn't have the luxury of grief or philosophical pondering.

"What do I think of what?" she asked.

Finn tossed a small pebble at her. "Don't tell me you were sleeping," he said, grinning at her.

Rommy felt an answering smile tug at her mouth. "I wasn't," she said and threw the pebble back at him. She rubbed at her forehead. "My thoughts, they just won't stay in order."

Finn's expression softened. "That's no big surprise. If you're half as tired as I am, you could sleep standing up. But, as much as I'd like to conk out for a month of Sundays, we've gotta move fast." He looked at the eclectic group gathered around the fire. Besides Little Owl and Alice, four fairies perched in various places.

Rommy noticed that Nissa was on Alice's shoulder, stroking the little girl's hair. "What I was saying is that we need to get that key, and the sooner the better. I don't know what Pan will do, now that he knows what we're up to, but I doubt he'll just sit back and do nothing. I wouldn't put it past him to use your friend Francie to keep us here."

Rommy jerked her eyes away from Alice and the lavender and silver fairy. She rested her chin on her up-drawn knees. "I think you're probably right, but my head feels fuzzy." She turned to the older woman. "Little Owl, do you truly think Tinkerbell has the key?"

Little Owl frowned. "She seems the most likely," she said. "If the key is not with Tinkerbell, I do not know where it could be hidden." She tapped her mouth with a forefinger. "It is possible that the fairy queen might have it in her own nest. Tell me again what Unilisi showed you."

Rommy thought back to the vision that Unilisi had flashed into her mind. The ancient tree being was the source of Neverland's magic, and they had had to travel through the jungle to reach her. Even then, there had been no guarantee that the tree would tell them anything. Fortunately, their journey was successful.

Rommy described the nest-like space Unilisi had shown her. It had reminded her of a rook's nest, with so many shiny little pieces. The nest appeared to be inside a tree, the bark an odd copper color.

"Did you see any other nests?" Little Owl asked.

Rommy shook her head. "It was huge and messy, but it was just one nest. I'm sure of that."

"That does not sound like the fairy queen's royal home, and the fairies nest in a community. Even the queen has ladies-in-waiting nearby. Plus, the color of the bark—the fairy tree has silver bark. I think it must be Tinkerbell's nest."

Nissa buzzed up from Alice's shoulder to hover near Rommy. "She will be dangerous to approach, after spending all this time alone. Her mind will be most unwell."

Rommy wrinkled her nose. "Why does being alone cause such problems for fairies?" she asked.

Balo, crossing his arms across his tiny chest, said, "Our magic must flow through all of us." When Rommy still looked confused, he rolled his eyes. "When it doesn't flow out, the magic backs up and poisons the user. Magic is meant to move in and out, not get stopped up like a cork in a bottle. Too much pressure and things tend to..." he gestured with his hands, miming an explosion.

Little Owl nodded. "It's true," she said. "Lone fairies become...feral."

"But even if she is feral, what can she do to us? Surely, we can overpower one small fairy if we have to," said Rommy.

Balo flung out his hands. "I can't believe I agreed to go on this harebrained trip with someone who knows so little. What can she do, you ask?" He spluttered to a stop and shook his head.

Nissa glared at him and then turned to Rommy. "Fairies have strong magic, even ones that have gone feral," she said. "If Tinkerbell's magic has built up, it could be quite...violent. She can do much more damage than mere size would suggest."

Kalen and Talen, the brother and sister warrior fairies, had been quietly sitting on either side of the door. Both of them straightened. "Someone is coming," said Talen.

Before any of them could respond, the door flap opened and Chief Hawk Eye ducked through. He straightened, his long sheet of black hair falling past his shoulders. He narrowed his eyes at the group arranged around his mother. One black eyebrow lifted.

Instead of getting flustered, Little Owl smiled. "Son, I am so glad you are here," she said, motioning with her hand for him to join them.

"Mother, I told you we must not be involved in this," said the Chief. "Captain Hook and our people have agreed to a truce, but if he finds we've helped his daughter on one danger-ous quest and are now helping her start another? I fear that the truce will no longer hold against his anger."

Little Owl stood up and walked over to the tall man. "Nonsense," she said, tapping his arm with a forefinger. "If these children complete their quest, Captain Hook will leave here, and he should be grateful, too."

Chief Hawk Eye looked at the ragtag group sitting in his mother's home and frowned. "I doubt his first feeling will be gratitude, but I guess we will see. I came to tell you he is on his way here right now. If you are still here when he arrives, I will not lie for you." His eyes searched each face.

Rommy shot to her feet. "Papa's coming here? Now?" She twisted her hands together. She hadn't seen her father since she and Alice had sneaked off his boat before he could take her back to London. "He mustn't find us, not yet. If he does, this quest won't even get started." Rommy looked at Little Owl with wide eyes.

Before Little Owl could say anything, there was a commotion outside. They all froze, their eyes fixed on the door of the tent.

"Chief Hawk Eye, I know my daughter is here. If you do not hand her over to me right this instant, you will be more sorry than you can imagine. Do you hear me?" the voice bellowed.

Chief Hawk Eye looked at Rommy. "I will go talk to him," he said. His dark eyes met Rommy's hazel ones. "I suggest you find another place to be." Then, he winked.

As Chief Hawk Eye turned to leave the tent, Little Owl motioned Finn, Alice, and Rommy toward the back wall. "Hurry, children," she said. "You must hide so that he doesn't find you."

Pulling up a wooden stake, she lifted one section of her tent. Alice wiggled through first, followed by Finn. Rommy squeezed Little Owl's hand.

"Thank you," she whispered before dropping to her knees to follow the others. Little Owl let go of the material and turned toward the door, her body blocking Rommy's legs as she pulled herself outside.

Rommy heard the swish of the door and then her father's voice boomed into the space. "Don't try to fool me, old woman. I know you know where they are."

Chapter 2:
Daughter Guilt

Finn and Alice were waiting for Rommy when she pulled herself to her feet. Finn nodded his head toward a group of rocks some distance away.

"We should get away from here," he said, his voice soft.

Rommy shook her head and tipped it toward the voices.

Both Finn's eyebrows disappeared under the fringe of his shaggy hair. "Are you daft?" he hissed.

"You go," Rommy said. "I want to hear what Papa has to say."

Alice tugged at her hand and pulled Rommy down until she could whisper in Rommy's ear. "Don't be a git. If your old man catches us, we're done for."

Rommy shook her head again and pushed Alice toward Finn. "You hide. I'll follow in a minute."

Finn huffed, paused, but took Alice's hand and moved away. The lamplight clearly outlined her father's and Little Owl's silhouettes.

Rommy crouched down and put her ear closer to the side of the tent. While she had to strain to hear Little Owl's soft voice, her father's came through loud and clear.

"Captain, Captain," said Little Owl, "you must calm yourself."

"Calm myself? Calm myself? Woman, my daughter just
disappeared off my ship, and I have no idea where she is. I don't
know if that brat Peter Pan has her, or if she is lost somewhere,
but I have a feeling you know exactly where I can find her." Her
father's voice had risen to shouting level.

"You do not give your daughter credit, Captain. She is
more clever and capable than you realize," Little Owl said.

"She is a child, and she doesn't know this place, how dangerous it is. Yet, you...you keep helping her. Every time something happens, I find YOU in the vicinity. Can you tell me why
that is?" A loud thunk meant her father had dug his hook into
something.

Amazingly, Little Owl chuckled. "Fathers do not want to
let their daughters grow up, but it is like trying to stop the tide.
Your daughter has a destiny, and not even you can stop it."

"I can bloody well try," her father bellowed. "Rommy can't
continually put herself into danger. I won't allow it!" His voice
faltered and became choked. "I can't lose her. I just can't. You
don't understand."

Was her father crying? In front of Little Owl? Guilt
speared through Rommy. She wanted to tell him she was fine,
but she pressed her lips together to keep the words locked away.

"I understand more than you think, Captain," said Little
Owl. "You've known great loss, but holding onto your daughter
so tightly will not keep her close. Like water, she will spill out of
your grasp. Water can only be held in an open, cupped hand."

Her father cleared his throat. She imagined him straightening his shoulders, pushing his black hair back. When he spoke

again, his voice was hard. There was no sign of the emotion from the moment before.

"Water needs to be restrained, or it will just dribble away. I don't plan on letting that happen to Rommy. Now, tell me where she is. So help me, if that boy is with her..." Something hit the ground.

Little Owl's voice lost some of its gentleness. "I understand you're upset, Captain, but you will not destroy my home. As you can see, neither your daughter nor her friends are here. Breaking my things will not change that."

Her father let out a loud harrumph. "But you know where I can find them, don't you?"

Her father's tone made Rommy feel nervous for Little Owl. Her father wouldn't hurt an old woman, would he? The truth was that while once she would have said no with confidence, she wasn't sure anymore. Since coming to Neverland, her father was different. As if in answer to her thoughts, Little Owl cried out. Rommy clapped a hand over her own mouth to stop her gasp.

Another deep voice rang out. "Take your hands off my mother, Captain." It was Chief Hawk Eye. Rommy bit her lip. This was all her fault. She was causing all this trouble for Chief Hawk Eye and Little Owl, who had been nothing but kind to her. But what could she do?

If she revealed herself now, there would be no quest. Her father would lock her up on his ship and set a 24-hour watch on her. She'd never get away. Pan would continue to kidnap children, and her father would continue his fruitless quest for revenge.

"I'll unhand her when she tells me where my child is," her father's voice snarled through the darkness.

"You will unhand her now." Chief Hawk Eyes voice was implacable.

"It is all right, Son," said Little Owl. "The Captain is not himself. I do not know your daughter's whereabouts, and that is the truth."

There was a crashing sound inside, and in the silence that followed, Rommy's gasp was loud.

"Ha! I knew she was here."

Rommy darted away from the tent and into the darkness beyond. The lavender moon was just a sliver in the sky, and its illumination wasn't enough to keep her from stumbling. She tripped over a root and went sprawling into some tall grass. She had barely gotten her breath back when an arc of light flashed over her head.

"Andromeda? I know you're out here," said Hook, his voice a shout. "It's time to stop this nonsense and come back with me."

She twisted her head. Her father was holding up a lantern, shining its light into the darkness. He was only a few yards away. She held still, hardly daring to breathe. The light moved away from her, and she lifted her head. The rocks where Finn and Alice were hiding were about six feet away. At their base was a tangle of bushes. They were big and dense enough that she thought she could hide in them. If she could just get there.

"Rommy? Darling?" her father's voice was softer, persuasive. "Come now, my dear, we can settle this together."

She bit her lip and pressed herself into the ground. His footsteps moved away, as he continued calling her name.

Glancing over her shoulder, she could see he was walking around the back of the tent. His back was toward her, but for how long?

An owl hooted in the darkness, and she slithered forwarded about a foot. Another call echoed into the night, and she pushed herself forward again. She was almost to the bushes. Suddenly, there was the sound of something hitting a tree on the other side of Little Owl's tent. Her father's footsteps hurried in that direction.

Rommy scrambled toward the bushes, pushing into their center. She ignored the branches that scratched at her face and pulled at her hair. Just kept pushing until her back was against the rock and a tangle of leaves closed in front of her. She rolled herself into a tight ball, squeezed her eyes shut, and prayed.

A moment later, footsteps moved her way. Light hit the back of her eyelids and she opened her eyes a sliver. Her father's boots stood not two feet away from her. She held her breath and waited. Hopefully, Finn and Alice wouldn't get caught. She hated to think of how her father might treat them.

"Where are you, Rommy?" There was a pause. "Please, I'm not angry with you. I need to know you're safe."

Rommy pushed her fist against her mouth and felt tears prick her eyes. Finally, the boots moved off in a different direction. She let out the breath she was holding.

"Oh, Papa," she whispered into the darkness, "If only I could trust you."

Chapter 3:
Making Plans

O ver an hour later Rommy determined it was safe to crawl out from her hiding spot. She had a cramp in her left calf and a crick in her neck. Alice and Finn were waiting for her as she straightened.

"I never thought he'd leave," said Alice. "I'll say this for yer old man, he's as stubborn as a mule."

Rommy gave a half-smile. "Yes, James Cavendish is nothing if not persistent." She motioned with her hand. "Come on, we need to talk to Little Owl."

The trio trooped back into Little Owl's home. Rommy found she could hardly look at the older woman, remembering how her father had behaved. Little Owl seemed to read her mind and came to stand in front of the younger girl.

"Do not worry, Child. I am well," she said. She smoothed a hand over Rommy's hair, pulling several leaves from it. "I see you have been communing with nature." She chuckled.

Rommy's cheeks reddened, but she smiled back. "Yes, I did spend some quality time with some brush tonight."

Finn straightened from where he had been slouching by the door. "I know everyone's tired, but we need to figure out how to get that key."

Little Owl shooed them toward the fire. "Sit. You all look like you are ready to fall over," she said. She pulled a jar from a shelf and poured liquid into several wooden cups. "Here, drink this and refresh yourselves. Then we will plan."

The three sat down on the soft blankets that Little Owl had placed there for that purpose. Rommy sipped the drink and found it cool with a minty flavor. After several swallows, a bit of energy seeped back into her, and she was grateful.

Alice leaned against her and yawned. "I'm so knackered, I could sleep standing up in a broom closet," she said. Rommy understood how Alice felt, but she pushed her own exhaustion away. They couldn't wait to begin this quest, and none of them would get much rest until they finished it.

She looked up at Little Owl who was in her rocking chair. The fairies, who had scattered when Hook and his men had arrived, had settled around the older woman. They glowed with their individual tints of color—amber, lavender, ice blue, and palest green.

"I believe you will find Tinkerbell on the far west side of the island," said Little Owl.

Alice scrunched up her nose. "If nobody's seen this fairy, how do you know where she is?"

Little Owl smiled. "That is a good question. When Rommy was describing the nest, she said there was copper-colored bark. There is only one tree on the island with that color bark, and that is the Old Willow. And the Old Willow is on the far west side of the island on a finger of land called the Salt Marshes that juts out into the sea."

Finn grimaced. "That's not good news," he said, his mouth tight.

"What do you mean?" asked Rommy.

Finn pushed to his feet and began to pace, his drink forgotten on the ground. "The Salt Marshes are dangerous," he said. "Not only are there boggy areas where people just disappear, but that's where the grommins live."

"Grommins?" Alice lifted her head from Rommy's shoulder and stared at Finn. "Don't tell me it's some plant thing that'll try to eat us!"

One side of Finn's mouth lifted. "No, they aren't killer plants." The smile slid from his face. "But they are just as dangerous."

"Well, what are they?" Rommy asked.

"They're swamp cats," said Finn. "They're not big, but they have poison in their claws and their teeth. It makes you hallucinate, and if they get you, you're a goner out there in the marshes."

Balo let out a huff. "As usual, you are uninformed, Boy," he said. "Grommins are only dangerous if you *bother* them. In fact, they can be quite useful, if they're of a mind. They can sense where the bogs are, and they can chase off will-o-wisps."

Rommy let out a strangled sound. "Will-o-wisps—what in the world are those? They don't sound very dangerous."

"How you have not died yet is a mystery," said the small fairy, shaking his head. "Will-o-wisps lead the unsuspecting into the bogs where they are swallowed up. Every marsh has them. They're how it feeds itself."

Rommy made a face. "That's... that's horrible." She shivered. "I never knew something like a marsh could be so...so...blood thirsty."

Balo rolled his eyes. "And I suppose you never eat meat?" He huffed out a breath. "Humans! They conveniently forget they are carnivores, too."

Heat climbed up Rommy's neck. She'd never thought of it that way before. Alice poked Rommy's arm.

"This ain't helping us find that key, and I can't knock off till we figure things out."

"You're right, Alice," said Rommy. She turned toward Little Owl. "So, this Old Willow is in the Salt Marshes? If Tinkerbell has the key, and she's as crazy and dangerous as everyone thinks she is, how in the world do we get her to give it to us?"

"Tinkerbell left her fairy community because her heart was broken," said Little Owl. "Peter Pan chose a human girl over Tinkerbell, and fairies can become very," she glanced at the four fairies, "attached."

Nissa spoke up from her perch on the back of Little Owl's chair. "Sometimes, a fairy will form a heart bond with a human. I believe this is what happened between Tinkerbell and Peter Pan. When Peter chose someone else over her, he broke that bond. This is a very serious injury to a fairy, one that can be healed, but only within the fairy community." Nissa shook her head, sending her silvery lavender hair flying around her tiny face. "I fear what we will find in the Old Willow."

Rommy leaned toward the tiny creature. "How can we get Tinkerbell to help us? Or, if she won't help us, how can we get the key away from her?"

"It is a difficult task," said Nissa. Her face creased in a frown. She looked toward Balo. "Do you have any ideas?"

Balo shrugged. "Crazy fairies aren't my speciality," he said.

Little Owl rose from her chair and went to a shelf on the far side of the room. She pulled down a box, rummaged around, and then pulled out something. When she had seated herself again, she opened her hand. In her palm were several sparkling beads in a rainbow of colors. "Perhaps Tinkerbell will be willing to trade," she said.

Little Owl dropped the sparkling stones into Rommy's hand, who turned them over several times before pushing them into her pocket. As she shoved them down, her fingers brushed something crinkly. Frowning, she wiggled her hand a little deeper and touched what felt like leaves.

Confusion clouded Rommy's mind until suddenly, an icy wave of realization washed over her. They were the leaves Unilisi had given her when Rommy had been in the grove. She had had to run to get out before opening into the grove had closed back up. In her panic, she had shoved the leaves into her pocket. She hadn't thought of them since.

The room wavered in front of her, and she closed her eyes. Lobo's last moments of life flashed in front of her. She could have used one of those leaves to save him, and she hadn't.

Her forgetfulness had cost Lobo his life.

Chapter 4:
Nighttime Conversations

Rommy felt a touch on her arm, and her eyes flew open. Finn was looking at her with concern.

"Are you all right?" he asked.

Rommy jerked her hand out of her pocket and dropped her eyes, afraid Finn would see her secret.

"Um, no, I'm fine," she said. She gave a small smile. "I guess I'm just tired."

Finn gave her shoulder a squeeze. "We'll be able to rest soon," he said.

He nodded toward Little Owl who had drawn a map that would show them where the Old Willow was located. They decided to leave at dawn after they all got some much needed sleep.

It didn't take long until Little Owl had brought out more blankets for them and banked the fire. Alice's head had barely touched the pillow before she was asleep. Finn's soft snores weren't far behind.

But despite the exhaustion that seemed like a physical weight, Rommy's eyes were wide open because every time she closed them, she saw Lobo dying. Her hand strayed back to her pocket, and she fingered the leaves again. A tear leaked out and traced a slow path down her cheek.

My fault. Lobo is dead because of me. That thought kept running through her mind on an endless loop.

In the dim light, she could see Little Owl moving around. She forced her eyes closed but her thoughts wouldn't stop whirring. Her eyes opened again, and she let out a sigh.

"Can't you find sleep, Child?" Little Owl asked.

"No," said Rommy, sitting up, careful not to disturb Alice or Finn.

"You carry a heavy burden on your shoulders. It is not surprising that sleep flees from you. Come, sit by me for a little while."

Little Owl sat on her own bed and patted a spot next to her. Rommy rose to her feet, tiptoed over, and plopped down. Little Owl put an arm around Rommy, drawing her head onto her bony shoulder, her hand smoothing the girl's brown sugar-colored hair.

"Now, what is weighing on you?" said Little Owl after a moment of silence.

For a moment, Rommy was tempted to tell the older woman her secret. Surely, if anyone would understand, it would Little Owl. But fear clawed up and closed off the words.

Rommy shrugged her shoulders. "I don't know," she said. "I suppose it's a lot of things, and I'm just so tired." That, at least, was the truth. She looked into Little Owl's kind eyes, and words flooded out. "When I came to Neverland, I just wanted to find my father. I didn't expect all this." She threw out her hand. "Now we must do this dangerous thing, and I can't help but worry about Francie. If anything happens to her...or any of the others...I'll never forgive myself." Her voice dropped to a whisper. "What if I can't do it? What if... someone gets trapped here or someone else gets killed, like Lobo? It'll be all my fault." A soft sob escaped.

For a moment, Little Owl simply rubbed Rommy's back. When she spoke, Rommy could hear the smile in her voice. "It's not all up to you," said Little Owl. "Whether the others choose to take the risk and come with you is their choice. You are not responsible for anyone's death."

A fresh wave of tears spilled out. Little Owl didn't know how wrong she was. The older woman hugged her close and continued speaking. "You will accomplish your goal. I have not met a young girl so strong and determined in my many years."

"But I don't feel strong," said Rommy, her voice catching. "I feel like I don't have any idea what I'm doing, and I'm putting my friends into danger." She swiped at the tears running down her face. "What if...what if I make a terrible mistake? What if I can't do this?"

"Oh, Child, we all make mistakes," said the older woman. She clasped one of Rommy's hands in her gnarled ones. "Don't you see? Yes, you are leading this quest, and that has its own burdens, but you aren't doing this alone. Your friends are with you, and when each of you fall down—which happens to us all—you will help each other back up. You are right. Alone you wouldn't be able to do this, but you are not alone." A soft, surprisingly young gurgle of laughter left Little Owl's lips. "Unilisi would not have shown you how to close that passage if she did not believe you could accomplish it. And she believed that, not just because of the fierce warrior you are in here," Little Owl pointed a bent finger at Rommy's chest, "but because she saw the strength and bond between you and Alice and Finn and the fairies. I dare say she also saw the deep love you have for your father and the love he has for you—even if he struggles to show it in the way you need."

Guilt threatened to overwhelm Rommy, and she opened her mouth to confess, to tell Little Owl how mistaken Unilisi was, how some mistakes weren't fixable. Then the thought of the older woman's expression turning into horror trapped the words once more in Rommy's throat.

Little Owl cupped her cheek, a soft smile on her face. "I can see you doubt," she said, "but you will see. You will see that Unilisi was right to choose you and your friends to fulfill this quest."

Rommy squeezed her eyes shut and hung onto those words, desperately wishing they were true. She wasn't sure why Little Owl's answer meant so much, but the older woman's words felt like an anchor in a very choppy sea. The idea of leaving her behind when the time came made Rommy's heart ache.

Squeezing Little Owl's hand, she blurted out, "You have to come with us. Don't stay on this cursed island. Come back with us."

Little Owl pushed a lock of hair off of Rommy's face, her smile sweet. "No, I am too old to leave this island now, and there is no place for me in your world."

"That's not true," Rommy said, shaking her head.

"It is true. Do native peoples such as I and my son have a place in your society?" Little Owl's tone was gentle, but her words were like sharp pricks.

"Well...I don't...that is... no, but that doesn't mean you wouldn't have a place with us," said Rommy, her words faltering.

"I know you mean well, but there is no place for me as I am in your world, and I am too old to learn a new way," Little Owl said.

"But why did you come here to begin with? How did you ever learn about Neverland?" Rommy's eyebrows lowered, her forehead wrinkling.

"My father's grandfather saw a wave of water, white as milk, crash across our lands. It swept away all of our villages, and our people disappeared under that relentless water. It is why our tribe came here, to save us and to preserve our way of life." Little Owl shook her head, the smile replaced by a frown. "But as you can see, that only lasted so long. Unlike the children here, we age—more slowly, but we grow old. We get sick. We die. This is all that is left of my people, and we grow fewer every year. It is why Tiger Lily is so restless and her heart so willing to follow Peter Pan."

"But...but...I don't understand," Rommy said.

Little Owl's eyes were sad, and she shook her head. "None of the other tribes would listen to my great-grandfather." She looked past Rommy. "My grandmother told me her father and the other tribes did not get along, and they did not trust him." She shook her head again. "It is as my great-grandfather saw—all the people swept under that wave."

Rommy put her hand over Little Owl's. "I'm so sorry," she said. "But I wish you'd reconsider and come with us. We can *make* a place for you, and for Chief Hawk Eye. Surely people would come to look past the differences and learn how wonderful you both are."

"You are very young still," said Little Owl. "People see what they want to see, and not always what is right in front of them."

Rommy threw her arms around the older woman who patted her back. Rommy noticed the pause before Little Owl spoke again. "Perhaps, though, my granddaughter is not too old to forge a new life, even in a difficult place."

Rommy drew back. "Tiger Lily?" she asked, her eyes wide. "Of course, she could come with us, I think. But...but...I don't...well, that is I doubt she'd want to. Would she?"

The smile was back on Little Owl's face. "We shall see."

The older woman pushed to her feet and looked down at Rommy. "You should try to sleep now," she said. "Morning will come too early, and you have a difficult task in front of you." Seeing Rommy's frown, she smiled. "But do not forget—you are not alone, and it is your bond that will give you all strength."

Rommy stood, and with a last hug for Little Owl, made her way back to her spot on the floor. She pulled the blanket up around her chin and determinedly pushed the guilt down deep. This quest was bigger than she was, and they needed to work together. That was why nobody could know about the leaves. She'd make sure she wouldn't let anyone down again.

Chapter 5:
On Their Way

FINN, ALICE, AND ROMMY alighted onto the scrubby grass, the fairies coming to hover around them. They were standing on the edge of the Salt Marshes, and the sun cast long shadows along the glistening ground.

The group had left as the first rays of dawn streaked across the sky, coloring it in pinks and yellows. Little Owl had made sure they were well-supplied, and even Chief Hawk Eye had come to see them off.

Their flight to the west side of the island had been uneventful but had taken much of the day. Rommy had spent most of the flight pushing away all thoughts of the silvery leaves that now felt as heavy as rocks in her pocket.

To distract herself she had watched the landscape which changed the further west they flew. The tall, waving grasses gradually gave way to rockier soil covered in short scrubby grass with an occasional twisted pine tree poking toward the sky. The river that ran so straight and strong on the east end of the island began to slow as they got closer to the opposite coast. It branched off into small channels until it disappeared into the marshes in front of them.

The group stared out across the boggy ground. Even with the sun still shining, there seemed to be a perpetual cloud of gloom that hung over the area. Rommy wasn't sure what she expected, but she saw no sign of a copper-colored willow tree, and a trickle of unease crept up her spine. Just how big were the Salt Marshes, and what was in there?

"Are we going to stand here all day, staring at a bunch of grass and water?" Alice asked. "I'm so hungry, my ribs is talkin' to my back."

The spell of the marshes was broken, and Finn laughed. He reached out and yanked on one of Alice's braids. "Leave it to you to think about food," he said.

"Well, ain't you hungry?" asked Alice.

"Yep, I sure am," he said. "And we may as well eat while we talk about how we're going to get to Tinkerbell."

The group retreated from the edge of the marshes. It didn't take long for them to dig out something to eat from the packs they carried.

The fairies, who didn't seem to eat often, simply perched around the three humans. "How far is it to this Old Willow?" Rommy asked, looking at Nissa and Balo.

"The Salt Marshes are bigger than they look," said Nissa. "That is one of their dangers. The journey seems short, but then travelers get caught out in the dark."

"I guess what you're saying is we shouldn't start across this late in the day?" Rommy asked.

Balo shook his head. "That would be about the stupidest thing anyone could do." He glared at her, and Rommy bit back a smile. The fairy with the golden topaz glow was perpetually grumpy. For some reason, it made Rommy want to laugh, but she stifled it so as not to hurt the fairy's feelings.

Finn swallowed his bread and said, "We should probably make camp tonight and start early in the morning. Balo's right. We don't want to get caught out on the marshes at nighttime. Like Nissa said, it's not safe. A lot of the dangerous critters come out after dark, not to mention the will-o-wisps."

Alice looked around at the empty space and shivered. "Are you sure it's safe out here? I feel like eyes is staring at me."

Rommy admitted to herself that all that open area made her nervous, too. She felt exposed, and there was a heavy silence that was only broken by the buzzing of insects.

Finn pushed to his feet. "Balo and I will go scout out some wood so that we can build a fire," he said.

"How am I supposed to carry wood?" complained Balo. "Do I look like I can carry wood?"

Finn just laughed. "I just need another set of eyes, Balo," he said. "Although, it wouldn't hurt you to carry some twigs."

The fairy harrumphed and followed Finn as he lifted off and headed back toward the closest pine tree.

"I ain't got a good feeling about this place," said Alice. The little girl looked around her and hunched her shoulders, as if trying to disappear into the prickly grass.

"We only have to stay long enough to get that key, and then we can leave," said Rommy.

"Yeah, but we gotta try to outfox mermaids who want to kill us," said Alice. She put her chin in her hands. "Danny and his gang were bad, but this place makes London seem like a walk in Hyde Park."

Rommy reached out and squeezed the little girl's shoulder. "Are you sorry you came?" she asked.

"Nah," said Alice. "I just hope we all make it off this island in one piece." She bounced up and looked at Rommy. "Should we start setting up a place to sleep?"

Rommy looked at the sky. While the sun was lower, she doubted it was much past late afternoon. She looked around at the empty landscape. Besides arranging their blankets, she wasn't sure what else they needed to do. There wasn't anything around here that could be used to build a shelter. Finn and Balo would be lucky to find enough wood to start a fire. She shivered. She just hoped it would last all night. She didn't want to speculate about being out here in the dark without a fire to keep away any of the creatures that roamed when the sun set.

ROMMY WAS JUST CONSIDERING going to look for Finn when she saw a golden brown glimmer. By this time, the sun had mostly set, and twilight had fallen like a dark cloak. Rommy didn't want to admit how relieved she was to see them.

Finn sauntered up to their campsite. Alice and Rommy had put out their blankets, and, with nothing else to do, were sitting there cross-legged. Finn held a pathetic amount of sticks and twigs in his arms. She eyed it skeptically.

"Do you think that will last all night?" she asked.

Finn shrugged. "It should if we keep the fire small. We'll also take turns keeping watch. We can't be too careful."

Kalen and Talen came to hover in front of Rommy. "We will keep watch, as well," said Talen, the sister of the sibling duo.

"But don't you need to sleep?" Rommy asked.

"We will take turns," said Kalen. His voice was surprisingly deep for his small size. Even after traveling with the two all the way into the heart of the jungle and back, Rommy had barely heard Kelan say two words.

She nodded at him. "We'll take turns, too," she said. "Well, Finn and I will. I don't think Alice needs to keep watch."

"Whadda ya mean? I can keep watch!" said Alice, planting her hands on her hips.

Finn looked up from where he was arranging the wood for the fire. "You don't need to worry about that, short stuff," he said.

Alice glared at him. "I ain't some baby you have to swaddle, you know."

"Of course not," said Rommy, trying to soothe the little girl's feelings. "If we need you, we'll definitely wake you up."

Alice frowned but reluctantly nodded her head.

By this time the sun had truly set. Neverland's pastel-colored stars were winking awake, their distant song flowing in the soft wind.

A screeching sound made them all jump.

Balo snorted. "That's just a bog owl," he said.

"Still, I better get this started," said Finn.

It wasn't long before a small fire was crackling. The three of them drew close to the fire, but Rommy still felt like anything could sneak up on her from behind.

Then she noticed the balls of light that had positioned themselves around them. Looking closer she realized that each of the fairies was facing out toward the blackness that surrounded them on all sides.

Alice had gradually inched closer and closer to Rommy, and now she was sitting almost in Rommy's lap. She put her arm around the younger girl. "We'll be fine, Alice," she said. She pointed at the fairies. "Nissa, Balo, Kalen, and Talen are keeping a good eye out."

"You think so?" Alice looked around.

Finn's teeth flashed white from across the fire. "You bet," he said. "Ain't no better lookouts than fairies. They can see like cats in the dark."

Rommy felt some tension leave the little girl, and she turned around and dug into her bag. "Maybe we should eat and then get some sleep. We should leave at first light so that we have time to get to that willow and back before it gets dark again."

Finn nodded his agreement. Both He and Alice dug through their bags, and soon the only sound was that of chewing.

Rommy tried to relax. The fairies had her back, but as she looked at Finn and Alice, and then out into the blackness that was no longer silent, she dreaded the long night ahead.

Chapter 6:
Into the Marsh

Rommy wasn't sure what woke her up. Clouds had scudded across the moon, leaving the night pitch black. Despite the darkness that pressed all around her, she immediately knew they were not alone. Before her eyes could search out the reassuring glow of the fairies, she felt a finger trail down her cheek.

Without thinking, Rommy rolled hard toward the touch. She felt contact and heard a satisfying oomph. Springing to her feet, she pulled out the dagger that was strapped to her side and yelled Finn's name. She heard him scramble to his feet, but it was still too dark to see much of anything.

The crowing laugh made her blood run cold, confirming who their attackers were.

"Such a shame you're a light sleeper," said Pan. "I was enjoying watching you. So peaceful."

Rommy shuddered but kept a firm grip on her dagger. "I'm not so peaceful now, though, Pan."

The clouds parted, and the sliver of moon illuminated what she had feared. Peter Pan and four Lost Boys surrounded them. Finn was holding off two of them and had Alice behind him. The younger girl wasn't just watching, though. She used her small size and speed to dash out, tripping one boy and kicking another in the back of the knee.

The one thing Rommy didn't see was the glow from the fairies. In the back of her mind, worry began to simmer, but she couldn't concentrate on that now. She had to hold off Pan, who was holding his dirk in front of him, casually examining the hilt like he'd never seen it before.

He looked at her and smirked. "Always ready for a fight, aren't you, Rommy? In that way, you're just like your old man." He tsked and shook his head. "Now, I'm not here to cause trouble, I just came to invite you to join me." He leaned forward, his smirk turning into a grin. He winked. "You know you want to."

Rommy leaned away from him. "You seem to have trouble understanding the word no," she said. "No matter how many times you ask me, the answer will always be no." She kept her dagger in front of her. She didn't take her eyes off Pan, even though he was hovering cross-legged and his dirk was loose in his hand. From experience, she knew he was unpredictable. And fast.

She glanced at Finn and Alice out of the corner of her eye. Finn was holding off the two Lost Boys who remained standing. The two others were sitting on the ground, holding their heads.

"Oscar, what do you want with him, anyway?" Finn said. "You don't have to stay here. You can come with us."

"Aww, Finn, I ain't got nothing back there," said Oscar. He had stopped circling Finn. "At least here, I eats most of the time, and I never freeze." He rubbed his arms as if remembering the bone-chilling cold that could envelop London.

"I don't want to hurt you, Oscar, but I can't let you stop me neither," said Finn.

Pan's laughter snapped Rommy's attention back to him. "Poor Finn," said Pan. "He always did have a hero complex." '

"Better than a villain complex," said Rommy.

Pan shook his head and smiled. Then he launched himself at her like a coiled snake. Rommy deflected the dirk and rose from the ground, flitting away from him. She missed her sword which was back at Chattingham's.

"That's what I like about you," said Pan, feinting at her. "You are always a good opponent. If you come with me, we'll never be bored." He came at her again with a flurry of strikes, which she just managed to hold off. If she hadn't been able to fly, she knew he'd have overpowered her. As it was, flight helped both with the height disadvantage and with her dagger's shorter reach. Still, she knew she could only hold him off. Winning this fight had much longer odds.

Lights at the corner of her eye caught her attention. The fairies—they were back. Before she could process what to do with this information, Pan came at her again. She dodged away from him, and Nissa came buzzing up to hover near her ear.

"We will distract them," she whispered into Rommy's ear. "You must head into the marsh and hide. Peter and his boys will not risk following you on foot."

Rommy gave a small nod to show Nissa she understood, but she didn't take her eyes off Pan, who was circling her, looking for an opportunity.

Nissa gave a sharp whistle, and Kalen flew up beside her. The two fairies began rubbing their hands together.

"Blast it!" said Pan when he saw the glow that was beginning to build between the fairies' hands.

"Pan!" called a high-pitched voice. "Pan, we're gettin' pelted."

"Come on," said Finn as he zipped past, Alice in tow.

Nissa and Kalen lifted their hands and shot twin glowing orbs at Pan who ducked. One sizzled across his tunic, leaving a scorch mark. He began backpedaling in the air.

Rommy retreated several yards before whirling and following Finn and Alice into the marsh.

"You'll never survive in there," Pan called after her. "You belong with me, Rommy. You'll be sorry you didn't listen."

Two orbs zipped through the air again, and she heard Pan yelp, but she didn't look back. Instead, she strained her eyes to see Finn and Alice. Below her, the swampy ground was covered in patches of long grass that formed a maze-like trail through open areas of sand and pools of water. Fog swirled and eddied around the islands of grass, making it difficult to tell what was sand and what was water. She headed toward a patch of sand. After checking that it was indeed solid ground, she was about to touch down when a hand yanked her into a patch of grass. She lost her footing and fell against someone. Gasping she pushed herself upright and looked into Finn's scowling face.

"Are you tryin' to get yourself killed?" he said.

"I made sure it was sand, not water," said Rommy, pushing her hair out of her eyes and glaring at him.

"That's not sand," said Finn. "That's a bog. If you had landed there, it would have sucked you down. Once you start to sink, it's almost impossible to get pulled out again. It's like cement."

"Oh," she said. She rubbed her arm. "Well, you could have just said something instead of nearly yanking my arm out of its socket."

Finn sighed and rubbed the back of his neck. "Sorry, I just didn't want Pan to know where we are. He's not going to give up, you know. He'll just follow us in the air and wait until he can get to us."

Rommy threw up her hands. "That's just great," she said. "Now, we have to do the two things everyone told us not to do—go through the Salt Marshes at night and on foot, and we have to do it with Pan chasing us."

Before Finn could answer, Balo came zipping into the tall patch of grass. "We need to get deeper into the marsh. The others are holding Pan and the rest of the Lost Boys off, but we have to hurry."

Without even looking to see if they were following, Balo flew on ahead into the tall vegetation. Rommy and Finn looked at each other, and then Rommy started forward, Alice behind her and Finn bringing up the rear.

Rommy shook her head as she followed the glowing amber light ahead of her. She just hoped they'd all make it back out again.

Chapter 7:
Grommins and Will-o-Wisps

They hadn't gone more than a few yards when Rommy started to see what looked like tiny floating jellyfish. They didn't sing exactly, but they hummed. As they moved, they undulated, almost like they were beckoning you closer. She lifted her hand to touch one that hovered in front of her face, but Balo zoomed back and smacked her hand.

"Don't touch those!" he said.

"But they're so pretty," said Rommy. "Maybe they can help us."

"That's a will-o-wisp, and the only thing it'll help you with is dying a nasty death in one of those bogs," he said. Then he turned to the light bouncing gently in place and began flapping his hands. "Shoo," he said. "Shoo, I say."

The light slowly floated away, its hum gradually fading.

Rommy clenched her hands to still their trembling. While there was so much beauty on Neverland, she wouldn't be sad to see the last of it.

Balo made an impatient gesture, and she continued after him, her boots squishing in the soggy ground. Eventually, she noticed that Nissa, Kalen, and Talen had rejoined them. The fairies took up their places, one on each side with Kalen behind Finn.

It was slow going as the trio pushed forward through the mud, following Balo's golden brown glow through the tunnel of grass. Balo's progress was in fits and starts as he determined the safest way to go. Even in the grassy areas, there were spots where they could sink up to their knees or worse.

Periodically, will-o-wisps floated into their path, but one of the fairies would shoo them away. Rommy could see how it would be easy to follow the lights.

Up ahead, Balo stopped and held up a hand.

"What is it?" she asked.

He put a tiny hand on her mouth and pointed upward. Rommy couldn't see anything because the grass really was like a tunnel, with the marsh's vegetation closing over their heads. She was just about to ask Balo what was going on when she heard Pan.

"Come out, come out, wherever you are!" he called. There was a pause. "What? You want to play hide and seek? All right—I'll be it. Ready or not, here I come."

A swooshing sound came from overhead, and the fairies dimmed their glow. Rommy, Finn, and Alice crouched down. Rommy felt Alice's arms go around her waist. The little girl was trembling. She felt a pang of guilt. If anything happened to Alice...

She felt Finn's hand grasp hers, and she squeezed back. She strained her ears. Was Pan still above them, or had he moved on to another part of the marsh? She hoped he got bored and lost interest soon. The mud on her boots was seeping into her pants, making them wet and cold. She shivered.

They waited a moment more, and then Nissa flew to Rommy.

"We will scatter around the marsh so Peter Pan cannot know exactly where you are. We will meet you at the Old Willow. Try to move as carefully as you can so he cannot see you from above."

Nissa, Kalen, and Talen zipped off in three different directions, and Balo signaled them to move forward again. Rommy followed but listened for any sound from Peter Pan. She couldn't hear anything but the night sounds of the marsh. For all she knew Pan was hovering right above her head.

This thought made her look up, trying to peer through the blades of grass curving above her head. She stumbled and almost fell.

Balo stopped and dimmed his glow until it was almost gone. He signaled for them to crouch down again, and then he flew off. Rommy's stomach felt like one big knot as they waited in the darkness for him to return. She slipped her hand into her pocket and fingered the leaves. Should she use them? She wasn't sure exactly what Unilisi meant when she had said the leaves were wishes. Could they make them all invisible? Rommy chewed at her lip, and then pulled her hand back out. The idea of everyone knowing she had magical leaves and had failed to use one of them to help Lobo made her stomach feel queasy. Besides, she didn't really know how the leaves worked. Then, Alice tugged on her sleeve.

"What is it?" she whispered.

Alice didn't say anything. She just pointed.

There were six pairs of yellow eyes ringed around them. A low rumble punctuated the air. The breath seemed to freeze in Rommy's lungs, and her eyes met Finn's.

"Grommins," he said.

At the same time, they both moved closer, sandwiching Alice more tightly between them.

"Balo!" she said as loud as she dared.

He reappeared, looking disgruntled until she pointed to the yellow eyes. It was just her, Finn, Alice, Balo, and the grommins, whatever they were.

A brown and cream dappled head broke through the grass not even a foot from where Rommy crouched. As the creature slid into view, Rommy felt some of her tension leave. It looked like a slightly bigger version of a house cat. Its fur was the same dappled pattern over its entire body, all except its tail, which ended in a pale yellow tassel of fur. The same yellowish fur hung in tufts from the ends of its ears.

The animal was rumbling, but it didn't seem angry or aggressive. Instead it sat down, its tail wrapping around itself. The animal cocked its head, looking at each of them in turn.

"So, this is what Pan is hunting in our territory—human younglings." It lifted a delicate paw and began to lick it.

The voice sounded feminine to Rommy, but she didn't say anything. Instead she looked at Balo, who moved to hover in front of the cat.

Balo gave a small bow and then spoke. "Neva, it is good to see you again," he said. "How is your family?"

Instead of answering, the cat gave a series of clicks, and with a rustle, five more cats slid into view. They were all the same brown and cream, although the patterns were slightly different on each one. While none of them were any larger than the first cat, Rommy started to feel a bit crowded. The tension had crept back into her shoulders because she remembered what Finn had said. They weren't big, but they were poisonous. Trust Neverland to have poisonous cats!

The cat nodded at Balo. "As you can see, they are well." She looked at Rommy and blinked at her and then back to Balo. "What are you doing with this group of younglings in the marshes?"

"We...that is to say..." he glanced at Rommy.

Tired of crouching, Rommy put one knee down into the squelching mud. She bowed her head as she had seen Balo do. "We did not mean to trespass," she said. "Originally, we were going to fly over the marshes to our destination, but, as you saw, Pan drove us in here. It is important that he not find us." Neva cocked her head and continued to stare at her. Rommy swallowed. "We are here to find the fairy Tinkerbell."

Neva rose and rubbed up against Rommy's knee. Then she rose on her hind legs, placed a paw on Rommy's knee, and gently batted at the stone hanging around Rommy's neck. Rommy's whole body tensed, but she didn't move away.

"A hearing stone," the cat said, her voice raspy. "That makes things easier." Dropping down to all four paws, the cat sat back on her haunches. "Do you realize that Tinkerbell's mind is sick? My family can lead Pan away from you, and I can take you safely to the Old Willow, but why go there? Once you get there, you might find more danger than in the marshes, certainly more than Peter Pan." A rumbling sound came out of the cat. Rommy wasn't sure if the animal was purring or laughing.

"We'd be very grateful if you could take us there," said Rommy.

The cat stopped rumbling and narrowed her eyes. "What is so important that you would brave the marshes and confront a feral fairy?"

Rommy hesitated and then decided to simply tell the truth. "We're looking for a key, and we think Tinkerbell has it. At least that is what Unilisi told me."

The cat's eyes flared wide for a moment. "You have spoken to the Tree Mother? You survived the jungles?" Then she gave an elegant shrug. "Then, I suppose you will survive the marshes."

Flicking her tail, the cat walked into the grasses and disappeared. Her family melted back into the vegetation. Rommy could hear a faint rustling in various directions.

Rommy and the others stared until Neva poked her head back. "Are you coming, younglings? We must finish our journey before the sun comes up. I do not travel after daybreak."

Finn, Alice, and Rommy looked at each other and then at Balo, who nodded his head.

Finn shrugged at Rommy, and the three of them started off again following the yellow tasseled tip of Neva's tail. They hadn't gone more than two yards, when it seemed to vanish. Rommy halted, and Alice ran into her back.

"Whatcha stopping for?" she asked, peering around Rommy. "Oh—where'd she go?"

Suddenly Neva's head popped up from a pool of water off to the right. "Come, younglings," she said. "We will take the underground tunnels. Pan will not see you here, and they go almost to the foot of the Old Willow."

The three looked at each other. "We...that is...none of us can, um, breathe underwater," said Rommy.

The cat snorted, her rumbling growing loud. "I am a cat, not a fish. I can't breathe underwater, either. You must dive to the tunnel entrance." She waited patiently.

Finn and Rommy looked at each other. Rommy didn't want to offend Neva, but the idea of following her into some supposed tunnel underwater made her nervous—very nervous. Finn didn't look anymore at ease than she did.

Balo came to hover in front of Rommy. "What are you waiting for? Pan to use you for target practice?"

"I'm just not sure..." she trailed off, not sure how much she should say with the cat staring at them.

Balo frowned, but then understanding dawned on his tiny face. He buzzed closer to Rommy's ear. "You can trust Neva," he said. "She'd have killed you by now, if that's what she wanted."

Rommy looked at Balo for a long moment before finally nodding. She might not know this Neva, but she trusted Balo and his knowledge of the animals on Neverland. She gestured to the others.

"Let's go," she said.

Rommy felt Alice tense behind her. "I ain't going in no hole in the water," she said.

The cat clambered back out and stalked over to Alice. "Hold on to me, youngling. I will direct you to the tunnel. It isn't far."

Alice trembled, but Rommy squeezed her shoulder. She could hear Pan's laugh carrying on the breeze and knew he was coming back their way. They couldn't keep crouching and hiding in some bizarre version of hide and seek all night.

"Come on, Alice," she said. "We'll all go together. It won't be like the waterfall. This water is still."

Rommy slid into the water, which came up to her shoulder, and Finn followed. He held out his hand to Alice. "We'll all be together. Promise," he said.

Alice shook her head and stood rooted on the bank. "I ain't going," she said, crossing her arms over her chest.

Rommy looked at Finn. He stared back and lifted both hands. Neva paddled back toward them.

"Why are you waiting? We must go quickly before Pan returns." Neva looked toward the sky, her glowing yellow eyes narrowed. Her yellow tasseled tail flicked just above the surface of the muddy water.

Rommy tipped her head toward Alice. "She's terrified of the water," she said so that only Neva could hear her. "I don't know how we're going to get her in here without a struggle."

A low growl rumbled in Neva's chest. "We must be gone before Pan comes back, or he could follow us into the tunnels." The cat paddled back over to the bank, clambered out, and shook herself.

Alice took a wary step back from the dappled animal. Neva let out a guttural call. For a moment, nothing happened, and then Rommy saw the long grass sway slightly. Suddenly, Alice was tumbling into the water. She came up sputtering and coughing, her arms slapping at the surface. Rommy grabbed one arm and Finn grabbed the other, and together they helped Alice find her footing. The water came up to her chin.

Neva slid back into the water and Rommy saw two yellow tasseled tails disappear into the darkness.

Alice scowled at the cat. "Are you going to drown me next?" she said.

Underneath the water, her hands dug into Rommy's arm, and up close, Rommy could see that the younger girl's face had gone white.

Neva flicked the end of her tail. "We do not have time for timid cubs," she said. "This is how we help our more reluctant young get used to the water." The cat let out a rumbling purr and swam up to Alice and nuzzled her chin. "Come, you can hold on to me, and I will lead you," she said.

Alice shook her head, the scowl slipping off her face. "I...I...can't," she said, her lips trembling.

"You can, Alice," said Rommy. "You're already in here. Besides, Finn and I won't let anything happen to you, and Neva said she will be right next to you." She leaned forward. "We don't have a choice, Alice. This is the fastest way to the Old Willow, and we have to beat Pan there."

Alice pressed her lips together and lowered her eyebrows. "This is the second time Pan's made me get dunked," she said. "He better hope I never get the chance to return the favor."

Rommy squeezed her hand. "On three, Alice. We'll all go under together."

Neval treaded water next to Alice, and the little girl buried her hands in the cat's fur. Rommy counted, and when she got to three, all of them took a big gulp of air and dove under the surface.

The water was murky and choked with vegetation, but in less than a minute, they were going through a hole and surfacing into a tunnel. Strange glowing lines lit up its sides and ceiling. They pulled themselves up and sat on the edge. A few moments later, Balo flitted into the tunnel with them, spraying water from his wings.

Neva shook herself and started walking. The tunnel was tall enough for Rommy to almost stand up straight, but Finn had to walk in a crouch. The cat glanced over her shoulder and then sauntered ahead.

Rommy, Finn, and Alice, along with Balo, followed the tasseled yellow tail into the glowing darkness. Rommy just hoped they hadn't made a big mistake.

Chapter 8:
Under the Earth

The tunnel dipped and curved, and several times they came to a fork. Neva never hesitated but kept moving forward at a steady pace. Rommy followed close behind her, each of her steps squelching in the damp earth. At what seemed like regular intervals, they came to openings in the floor like the one where they had surfaced. Water lapped over the edges of these openings, but Neva would skirt it and keep going.

As she walked, Rommy started to dry off. The muddy water left a film of slime behind, making her clothes feel stiff, and her hair hung in clumped bunches, her braid long since undone. She was rather glad it was dark at the moment.

Alice had taken hold of the back of her shirt when they started walking and hadn't let go. She could hear the others' soft breathing, but, otherwise, it was silent in the tunnels. They just kept walking and walking into the glowing darkness.

Rommy tried not to think about the fact that if Neva left them, they'd be lost down here probably forever. She felt the press of the earth above her and focused on breathing in and out. Even if they turned and went back the way they came, she didn't think she could remember all the turns Neva had made. She shuddered. She still didn't know why the cat was helping them in the first place. Balo had said the grommins could be helpful, but why Neva had chosen to help them, she didn't know. Maybe Pan had made another enemy. He seemed to have quite a few of those.

After what felt like hours, they came to another opening like the one from which they had entered the tunnel. Unlike the others, this one didn't have visible water at its mouth.

Alice was already shaking her head. "I ain't going in no hole," she said.

Neva rubbed against the little girl's leg. "It is not like the one where you entered the tunnel, youngling. The tide is still out."

Alice reached down and stroked the cat's soft fur and she rumbled again. "There ain't no water down in there? You promise?"

"I cannot promise you won't get wet, but the tunnel is still dry yet. When the tide comes in, that is a different tale. Come."

Neva paused at the lip of the opening and looked at Rommy and Finn. "You must slide in and lie flat. If you sit up, something may hit your heads. Come, Alice, you will follow me."

Alice looked at Rommy, who nodded her head. "You heard Neva. Sit at the edge and slide into the opening."

The cat slunk into the hole and disappeared. Alice sat down and raised an eyebrow at Rommy. She scooted a bit further in, and suddenly she disappeared. Her shout echoed up after her.

Rommy slid her feet into the cavity and carefully eased down. She could feel the wetness seeping into her shirt as she shifted flat onto her back. She cautiously let go of the edge, and then she was flying.

Twisting and turning, she rocketed through the darkness until she shot through another opening and landed in waist-deep water. She spluttered to the surface just as Finn came sailing in and almost landed on top of her.

It wasn't until she was standing and wiping water from her face, that Rommy realized it was salty. They must be at the edge of the far end of the island where the marshes emptied into the ocean.

Although the moon was still only a sliver, compared to the darkness of the tunnel, it seemed almost bright. She could clearly see Alice standing in the middle of the salty pool grinning.

"Are you all right?" Rommy asked her.

"All right? That was bang up the elephant, that was," said Alice. "I didn't even mind the dunk at the end." Then she giggled.

Rommy grinned back. "It was quite the ride, wasn't it?"

Finn was shaking water out of his eyes, but he was smiling, too.

Neva had climbed out of the pool and was grooming herself. She paused and looked at them. Rommy wasn't sure, but she thought the cat smiled.

They all clambered out of the water and sat on the rocky sand on the edge of the pool. There were still patches of the long grass, but they had thinned out. At the very edge of the land stood an enormous willow tree.

Its bark glowed a dark red in the moonlight, and its long trailing branches shone gold. They were in Tinkerbell's front yard, so to speak. With a gasp Rommy felt in her pocket. Sighing with relief, she pulled out the colored stones that Little Owl had given her, careful to avoid the leaves.

Alice touched them and then looked up at her. "What are we waiting for? Shouldn't we go get that key from the crazy fairy?"

Rommy shook her head. "We need to wait for Nissa and the rest before we do anything," she said. "I'm not sure the best way to approach Tinkerbell." She looked at Finn, and then Balo. "You know the fairies better than I do, and you *are* a fairy. What do you two think?"

Balo scowled. "Why would I know what a half-cracked fairy would think?"

Finn shrugged one shoulder. "This is different," he said. "Tinkerbell isn't like the other fairies."

Neva stood up and stretched. "I wish you luck on your task. I must go rejoin my family."

Rommy walked over to the cat. "Thank you, Neva, for your kindness. I don't know why you decided to help us, but we are very grateful."

Neva rubbed herself against Rommy's leg and purred loudly. "I don't like Pan." The cat's eyes narrowed to slits. Her voice took on a hissing quality. "He likes to play games, and one of those games cost me a cub."

Rommy's eyes widened. "I'm so sorry, Neva."

Alice squatted down and hugged the cat. "That ole Pan, he's a right git."

The cat ran a sandpaper tongue over Alice's cheek. "You are sweet younglings. I wish you luck on your journey." Alice let Neva go, and the cat sauntered back toward the heart of the marsh. She glanced over her shoulder.

"One piece of advice," she called back. "Wait until the sun comes up before going to see the fairy, and if she seems happy, be watchful."

It only took a few moments until Neva melted back into the Salt Marshes.

"Whadda we do now?" asked Alice.

Rommy sat down on the rocky sand. "I guess we wait for the sun to come up."

Chapter 9:
Out of the Marsh,
Into the Frying Pan

Dawn had turned to morning when Rommy opened her eyes with a start, her chin slipping off where it had rested on her hand. Nissa hovered in front of her. Rommy looked around. Alice's head was in her lap, and Finn was stretched out on the sand with his arms behind his head. He cracked his left eye open and then sat up.

"I can't believe we all just fell asleep," he said.

"I know," said Rommy. She looked over at Balo, who was perched on a piece of driftwood with his arms folded across his chest. "It's a good thing we have someone like you to guard us."

Balo harrumphed. "With all your snoring, it's a wonder Tinkerbell didn't hear us and come out to see what all the ruckus was about."

"Never mind that," said Nissa. "We led Peter Pan to the far side of the Salt Marshes. I do not know if he will be fooled for long, though."

Kalen and Talen raised the tiny spears they always had with them. "We will stand guard outside the Old Willow while you reason with the fairy inside," said Talen.

"Thanks, Talen," said Rommy. "But how do you think we should approach her? Neva told us to wait until the sun was up. It seems the sooner we get this done and get out of this marsh, the better off we'll be. I'd rather not spend another night here."

"Me, neither," said Alice.

Finn stretched his arms overhead. "Maybe it would be best if only one or two of us goes to talk to her. If we all show up, she might feel like we're ganging up on her."

Rommy put a hand on his arm. "Finn, I think you and I should go. You have a natural affinity with the fairies, and maybe I can explain things to her." Rommy dug out the sparkling stones that Little Owl had given her, careful not to disturb the silvery leaves. "I hope these do the trick."

Nissa nodded and looked around. "I do not think we should approach her," she said, gesturing to herself and the other fairies. "Tinkerbell has chosen to leave our community. She can only see our coming as something ominous."

Rommy pushed to her feet and dusted off her pants. "Well, that's settled then. We'll go and talk to her."

Alice was staring at her.

"What?" Rommy asked.

"Um, I think you might want to," Alice waved her hand toward Rommy's hair, "... ya might scare her."

Rommy put a hand to her head and a large chunk of mud fell to the ground. Her face turned hot as she ran her hands through her hair. Dried mud and tendrils of slimy plants formed a shower of debris. "Oh, I...well..." She spun away from Finn, wishing she could disappear back into the tunnels.

Finn let out a burst of laughter. He bushed at his own hair and shook his head vigorously, sending dirt flying every which way. "I guess we're all kinda a mess. It was probably that marsh water that slicked us all up."

Alice pulled at Rommy's arm. "Sit down, and I'll help you," she said.

Rommy immediately dropped back to the ground. She felt Alice's fingers running through her hair. Once the other girl was done, Rommy reached up and quickly re-braided the still stiff strands, tying it with a piece of vine that one of the fairies handed to her. She went to squat next to the pool and splashed water on her face before standing up.

"Here," said Alice, reaching up and swiping at Rommy's ear. A glob of mud fell off onto the ground.

Rommy covered her face with her hands and gave a strangled laugh. "I didn't realize I had brought quite so much of the bogs with me."

Finn spun her around and scrutinized her face. She could feel the heat climbing back up her neck, but she tried to ignore it. "Well," she said, lifting her chin, "do I pass muster, or do I still look like a marsh monster?"

A smile tugged at Finn's mouth. "I think you look just right."

If her face got any hotter, Rommy thought it might burst into flames. She squared her shoulders. "Right, then. I guess we should go talk to Tinkerbell. Before it gets any later, I mean."

"I don't talk to big ugly girls," came a scratchy voice. "But I'll talk to you, Boy. I never get visitors no more."

Rommy and Finn whirled around to find a creature—Rommy had a hard time believing it was a fairy—hovering behind them. She had silver hair, but unlike the other fairies, instead of gently floating around her head, it writhed like Medusa's snakes. Her glow had perhaps been silver at one time, but now it resembled tarnished pewter. Rommy didn't think fairies got wrinkles, but Tinkerbell's face looked pinched and had a sickly yellow tinge to it. Her eyes were a dark blue, almost navy, and her white dress had turned a dingy gray and hung limply around her.

Rommy felt a pang of pity for the tiny fairy. Whatever had happened, it was clear time had not been kind to her, and she was not well.

Finn looked at Rommy and raised an eyebrow. Rommy nodded her head slightly. Finn smiled broadly at the fairy. "I'm Finn," he said, putting a hand on his chest and then gestured toward the fairy. "And you must be Tinkerbell?"

The fairy smiled and sashayed closer to him. She cocked her head and smiled. "And why have you come to see me, Finn?"

"I," he gestured toward Rommy, "and Rommy here were hoping you could help us."

Suddenly, Tinkerbell began to shake. Her hands and feet began to glow a dark red. Her eyes dilated until they looked black. "I don't help big dumb girls," she screeched. "I hate big dumb girls. They steal everything."

She flew at Rommy's face, her small hands looking like claws. "Get out! Get out of my marsh."

For a moment, Rommy just stared, and then her reflexes kicked in. She ducked out of the way of the infuriated fairy just as a ball of red light shot from the fairy's hands. It passed so close to the side of her face, she felt the heat.

"Hey," she said. "Knock it off! I haven't stolen anything from you."

"Yeah, and she's not dumb," said Alice.

Tinkerbell's face was twisted into a snarl. "What about him? You took him!" she hissed, pointing at Finn.

Rommy frowned. "You didn't even know him five seconds ago. How could I steal him? Besides, he's way too big to steal."

Tinkerbell opened her mouth, and then she started laughing. She laughed until tears ran down her tiny face. "Too big," she kept repeating.

Finally, the fairy straightened. "You are still ugly, but maybe you aren't dumb," she said. She cocked her head again. "What do you want? Nobody comes here unless they want something."

She flew closer to Rommy, who fought the urge to flinch. How to ask for the key so that Tinkerbell would agree? Should she mention Peter Pan or would that push the fairy over the edge again?

Finally, she decided on the truth—or part of it, at least. "We've come to see you because you have a key that will help us."

Tinkerbell's eyes narrowed, and she buzzed around Rommy's head like an angry bee. "Help you? How will it help you? Nobody knows about that key but the Tree Mother. Who told you I had it?"

"You're right. Nobody knows but Unilisi. She told me when I visited her in her grove," said Rommy.

The fairy started to vibrate again, and Rommy dug into her pocket and pulled out one of the sparkling stones. "We wouldn't expect you to just give it to us, but we brought something to trade." She held up the stone.

Tinkerbell's expression changed to one of wonder. She flew closer and put a hand on the glistening pink glass-like stone. Then her eyes narrowed again. "If I give you the key, what will you do with it?"

Rommy glanced at Finn. He widened his eyes. How much should she tell the fairy? What would convince her, and what would set her off?

"Why don't you show it to us first so that we know it's the right key?" suggested Rommy.

Tinkerbell snarled and began to shake again. Rommy quickly dug in her pocket again and brought out the green sparkling stone. She held it up next to the pink one. "Just show us the key, and I'll give you both of these."

Tinkerbell's mouth tipped up into a smile. She nodded once and clasped her hands together before turning and flying toward the copper-colored tree. After only a few feet, she whirled back around. "I thought you were only ugly, not dumb," she said. "Come on."

Rommy and Finn looked at each other and then at Alice, who shrugged. Together they followed the fairy as she flew in a looping path toward her nest. Nissa, Balo, Talen, and Kalen followed at a discreet distance, trying to stay out of Tinkerbell's line of sight.

Before they could catch up with her, she had reached the Old Willow and flown up under its long graceful branches. They stopped in front of those branches, not sure if they should get closer. A moment later, Tinkerbell reappeared.

In one hand, she held a long, glistening jade stick. It was the key.

Chapter 10:
Key to the Kingdom

Tinkerbell held out her other hand and snapped her fingers. Rommy edged forward and held the stones out to the fairy. They were far too large for the fairy to grasp, but Tinkerbell made a gesture and a glow rose from her palm, encompassing the two stones. Rommy let go, and they hovered over Tinkerbell's hand.

Without another word, she whirled and disappeared under the branches again. Rommy expected the fairy to return, but she didn't. Could she use one of the leaves to get that key without the others knowing? She inched her finger into her pocket and her fingertip brushed the edge of a leaf. If only she knew how they worked. Then, she might be able to use one without anyone seeing. She withdrew her hand. Rommy knew she couldn't risk Finn or Alice noticing the leaves or they'd start asking questions. They couldn't know her secret, or they would hate her. She shivered at the thought of being alone in Neverland and pushed the disturbing thought away. They could just wait for Tinkerbell.

Several minutes went by, and the trio looked at each other. Now what?

Rommy stepped closer. "Tinkerbell?"

Nothing.

She tried again. "Tinkerbell? We'd like to talk about the key."

Nothing.

Rommy turned toward Finn just as Tinkerbell came zipping out from underneath the tree's sweeping branches. There was a snarl on her tiny face.

"How do you know about the key?" she asked.

Rommy raised her eyebrows. Oh dear. The fairy was worse off than she had thought. Apparently memory loss was also an issue besides just plain craziness.

"Um," Rommy started.

Finn stepped forward. "We are here to see you, Tinkerbell. The Tree Mother told us you were the keeper of the key, and you were the only one who could help us."

The fairy's expression changed. She smiled, her eyes sparkling. She flew to hover in front of Finn's face. "You are right," she said. "I am the keeper of the key, but why should I help you?" She flew around him, and Rommy tried not to roll her eyes as the fairy batted her lashes at Finn.

Finn gave the fairy a grin and pushed the hair out of his eyes. "Because you can get back at Peter Pan and make him sorry he ever crossed you."

Tinkerbell's eyes got wide, and her hands started to turn a dull red. "Peter Pan must die," she said, her voice so piercingly high, Rommy clapped her hands over her ears.

"Gone 'round the bend, that one," she heard Alice murmur.

Finn shook his head. "We're going to do something better than kill him. We're going to make him suffer—forever."

It looked like steam was actually coming out of the tiny fairy's ears. Her eyes were almost black.

"Tell me," she said, pointing a finger at Finn.

To his credit, he didn't flinch, although Rommy thought she would have probably ducked if that glowing red finger was pointed at her.

"We're going to seal him in Neverland forever," said Finn. "He'll never be able to leave, and he'll be here all alone. You know Peter hates to be alone."

Tinkerbell let out a long cackle, bending over from the waist. When she straightened, she lifted her palms to the sky and let out two long blasts of red. When she stopped, smoke lingered in the air, and there was a distinct odor of sulfur. Slowly the fairy's hands and feet returned to a normal color.

Rommy felt Alice move closer to her. She didn't blame her. The fairy was unstable and dangerous—a bad combination to be sure.

Finn leaned closer to Tinkerbell. "Unilisi told us how to seal Pan away," he said. "All we need from you is that key."

Tinkerbell looked around, and her eyes stopped on Rommy. She pointed. "Not her," she said. "No big dumb girls. Make her leave, and we will do this together, you and I." She slid closer to Finn.

He didn't bat an eye. "We have to take the big dumb girl with us," he said. Rommy ignored the irritation that flickered.

Tinkerbell narrowed her eyes. "Why do we need her? All you need is me," she said, her voice purring. She placed her small hand on Finn's shoulder.

Finn shrugged. "Hey, it's not my idea," he said. "Unilisi gave the quest to her, don't ask me why."

Rommy's eyes flickered downward. She wondered why Unilisi had picked her to share the quest with. The Tree Mother must have known she would ruin it all. Maybe Unilisi didn't want Neverland to be sealed up.

Tinkerbell's high-pitched voice interrupted Rommy's thoughts. "The Tree Mother chose *her*?" Tinkerbell looked at Rommy, her lip curling. She let out a huff. "I suppose if we must take her..." she whirled back to Finn and held up a finger. "But, I keep the key until it's needed. I won't give it to either of you."

Without waiting for a response, Tinkerbell darted back under the branches and brought out the key. It was almost as long as she was, and Rommy wondered how in the world the fairy was going to carry it for any length of time. Before she could voice these thoughts, though, the fairy opened a small bag attached to her waist. She slid the key into it. Rommy blinked.

"How d'ya get that big thing into that teeny bag?" asked Alice, scrunching up her nose.

Tinkerbell let out a tinkling laugh. "My magic, of course," she said. She flew over to Alice and patted her cheek. Alice flinched away, and Rommy saw an expression pass over the fairy's face that almost looked like hurt. Then it was gone.

Rommy poked Finn and mouthed to him, "The other fairies?" and raised both her eyebrows. While the four fairies had blended into the background, they couldn't be expected to remain unseen for the rest of the quest.

Finn held up a hand to Tinkerbell. "We are traveling with others of your kind," he said. "They have agreed to help us in our quest and have been faithful companions." He gestured, and Nissa, Kalen, Talen, and Balo appeared.

Tinkerbell let out a shriek and zipped behind Finn's head. "Get them away from me! I'm not going back, and they can't make me."

Finn rubbed the ear that was closest to the fairy. "They aren't here to take you away," he said.

"Like we'd want you in the community," muttered Balo.

Nissa placed a hand on his arm and shook her head. She flew forward. "We have no wish to harm you or take you anywhere, Tinkerbell," she said, her voice soft. "Our only purpose is to help the humans. We have been charged in this quest. You may give Finn the key, and we will leave you here unbothered." Nissa placed a fist on her heart. "You have our pledge."

Tinkerbell slipped out from behind Finn, suspicion written clearly on her face. She wagged a finger at Nissa. "You aren't tricking me into not going," she said. She patted the bag at her waist. "I'm coming. Just don't bother me. You can stay in your community, but don't try to pull me back in." She said the word community like someone else would say toilet.

Nissa simply nodded. Balo crossed his arms and scowled. "We're going to regret this, mark my words," he said under his breath.

Tinkerbell darted forward and then stopped after several yards. She turned back to them, her hands on her hips. "Well, what are you waiting for? Don't we have some revenge to get?"

Rommy and Finn exchanged glances with the fairies. Nissa shrugged. At least Tinkerbell was cooperating. The trio lifted off the ground and followed the crazy fairy. Rommy didn't know whether to be happy they had the key or scared that things could go amazingly wrong with this creature along for the quest.

As if reading her mind, Alice piped up. "Well, this should be interesting."

Rommy couldn't help but agree.

Chapter 11:
Steps to a Successful Quest

When the group finally touched down outside the Salt Marshes, it was afternoon. Rommy scanned the sky for any signs of Peter Pan, and while she should have felt relieved, not seeing him made her nervous.

Alice gripped her hand. "I keep expecting *him* to show up. Least ways, iffen he was here, I'd be able to keep my eye on him," she said, echoing Rommy's own thoughts.

Rommy squeezed her hand. "I know," she said. "I'm afraid he might just pop up all of a sudden. We'll just have to believe our luck has turned."

"We ain't been lucky since we stepped foot on this island," said Alice. "I ain't never thought I'd say this, but I miss London."

"We have the first part of the quest done," Rommy said. "We'll be back before you know it." She didn't say she was unsure of what would happen to Alice when they returned to London. That is if they didn't get sealed here right along with Pan. Her Papa hadn't been too keen on Alice, and Alice didn't feel any more warmly toward him. Rommy sighed. She'd just have to cross that bridge when she came to it.

Finn drew closer to Rommy and Alice. "Well, we've got the key. Now what?" he asked, looking at Rommy.

"I'm hungry," said Alice. "I think the next thing we should do is eat something before I expire on the spot."

Finn smiled and messed Alice's hair. "Are you ever not hungry?"

Alice crossed her arms. "It's not like you ever turn down food," she said.

Finn laughed and his eyes met Rommy's. "Well? What do you think? We can eat and figure out what do next?"

"I think that's a good idea," said Rommy. "We have the key, sort of, but we have to be careful when we close the passage to give ourselves enough time to get everyone out."

Finn nodded and then looked around. "The problem is, what are we going to eat?"

Nissa, who had been hovering nearby, spoke up, "Balo and I can go get some marshberries." She nodded at Balo who simply scowled. The two of them flew off.

Tinkerbell stared at all of them. "What are you doing? We have to go, go, go," she said, her arms flying every which way.

"No, we need to figure out what to do next," said Rommy.

"I *know* what to do next!" said Tinkerbell, her eyes dilated and her hair writhing. "Get Peter Pan." Her tiny hands stretched out in front of her, and she twisted them like she was choking an invisible person.

Alarm zinged through Rommy. "No, Tinkerbell," she said. "We're going to seal Pan here so he can't leave Neverland. We aren't going to harm him."

Tinkerbell let out a long cackle, and then seeing Rommy's dismayed expression, she abruptly stopped. "Okay," she said.

She turned her back and perched on the petal of a delicate yellow wildflower.

Rommy, Finn, and Alice blinked at her before collapsing onto the ground in a circle. "Since we only have sunrise to sunrise to get everyone out of Neverland, we should get Francie and any Lost Boys who want to go first. Then we can turn that key," said Rommy.

Finn cocked his head. "I don't know," he said. "Once we take Francie and any Lost Boys, Pan is going to be on our tail even more than he is now."

"But if we leave it too late..." she shook her head. "I don't want to cut it too close, and don't forget I have to...persuade...Papa." She closed her eyes briefly, dread gathering in her stomach. "He's going to be so angry with me."

She felt a touch, and her eyes opened to find Finn's hand on hers. She looked up at him, and once again her eyes caught in his. A fizzle of emotion stretched between them.

Then Alice snapped her fingers near Rommy's face. "You've gone off your chump if you think yer old man is staying here if you leave," she said, her voice breaking the spell between Rommy and Finn.

Finn looked away and rubbed a hand on the back of his neck. Rommy could feel heat rising in her cheeks, and she cleared her throat.

"I don't know, Alice," she said. "He was so angry before, and this will be worse."

"Old Captain Hook might be a pirate, but he's your father, too," said Alice.

A loud screech made all three of them whip their heads around to find Tinkerbell vibrating in front of them, her arms and legs a fantastical fire-engine red. "Captain Hook?" she spluttered. "You're Captain Hook's daughter? I'm going on a quest with *Captain Hook's daughter*? No! No! I won't do it. I won't help that fiend." Her voice climbed so high and loud Rommy thought her eardrums might burst.

Finn put his hands out. "Hey, Tinkerbell, take it easy," he said. "You aren't helping Captain Hook. You're getting him out of Neverland. Forever."

"What about her?" Tinkerbell pointed a shaking finger at Rommy. "She's Hook's daughter. I'm not giving her my key. I'm going back to my nest."

Something in Rommy snapped. She was tired of this stupid island and feeling like she was at the mercy of these stubborn creatures. She stood up and moved in front of the angry fairy. "I might be Hook's daughter, but I'm the one who found out how to seal Pan on this island, and I'm the one who's going to get us all off of here, including Captain Hook. If you'd like to see Pan free to come and go as he pleases and let my Papa stay here forever, keep your key. Go back to your tree, and see if Pan even notices or cares."

Out of the corner of her eye, she could see Finn shaking his head. Even Talen and Kalen were staring at her, wide-eyed.

Tinkerbell glared at her for a long moment, and then she bent over double laughing. Balo and Nissa had flown up with their arms full of berries. They stopped and gaped at Tinkerbell, who was rolling one way and then the other, her loud laughter sounding like a crazed bell.

Finally, she stopped and wiped her eyes. She buzzed over to hover in front of Rommy's face. "You're the only one that isn't afraid of me," she said. She pointed around the circle. "The rest of them, they're all afraid of what I'll do because," she leaned in close and bared her small, pointed teeth, "I'm crazy. But not you." She let out a tinkling laugh again and then stuck out her tiny hand. "I'll help you." Rommy used one finger to "shake" on it. Then Tinkerbell gave a sly smile and winked. "But I'm still coming with you." She patted the bag at her waist. "And I'm keeping the key until you need it."

Chapter 12:
Anticlimax

Rommy and Finn crouched behind the rocks that marked the outskirts of Pan's hiding place. By the time they had gotten here and sneaked into position, a purply twilight lay over the island. In the semi-darkness, Rommy squinted but didn't see any movement.

It made her nervous.

She glanced behind her. Alice, along with Kalen and Talen, were secreted further away. Rommy didn't want to rescue Francie only to find Alice Pan's hostage instead. It hadn't taken much persuading for Alice to agree to stay behind.

Unfortunately, she hadn't been as successful with Tinkerbell. The fairy's eagerness sent a ripple of unease through Rommy. Despite Tinkerbell's agreement to help, she was a loose cannon. Rommy just hoped she would stick to the plan.

Rommy leaned closer to Finn. "Do you see anyone?" she asked.

Finn shook his head. "I don't think they're here." He cautiously stepped out from behind the rock, and Rommy grabbed the back of his shirt.

"What are you doing? What if Pan is just waiting to ambush us?"

Finn grinned. "Unless he can read minds, I doubt it." He shook off her hand and moved closer to the caves.

The rocks were still in a circle, but the campfire was completely out and looked like it had been for a while.

Rommy followed Finn as they walked around the deserted camp. Balo and Nissa dimmed their glow and flew into the various caves.

When they came out, they shook their heads.

"Nobody is here," said Nissa.

"They've left," said Balo, "and I don't think they are coming back." He let out a loud sigh.

Rommy looked at Finn. "What do we do now?" she asked. "Do you have any idea where Pan could be?"

Finn ran a hand through his hair. "Could be any number of places," he said, kicking a stone across the clearing. "No telling how long it'll take to find him. I should have known he'd get the jump on us." He kicked another rock, harder this time.

Rommy laid a hand on his arm. "It's not your fault," she said. "And maybe this is better. We all need some rest. We'll have more time to make a plan that's not as risky. Maybe this will help us in the long run."

Finn put his hand over hers. They looked at each other, both of them smiling.

"Thanks," said Finn. "You're probably right."

He shifted closer.

Rommy couldn't seem to look away.

He leaned forward, his eyes starting to close.

Rommy felt hers sliding shut, too.

A bright light buzzed between them.

"I know where he is!" said Tinkerbell. "When you two are done mooning over each other, I'll show you."

Finn and Rommy jerked apart.

Rommy's face felt like it was on fire, and Finn looked everywhere but at her.

Tinkerbell crossed her arms and tapped her foot in the air. "Well? What are you just standing there for? I said I know where Peter Pan is."

Rommy shook her head to clear it. "That's great," she said. "But I still think we should rest up before we go anywhere else tonight. I know I'm tired and everyone else has to be too—even you, Tinkerbell."

"I suppose I could do with a rest," said Tinkerbell slowly and then whirled in a circle. "But not before I tell you where he is." She zipped back and forth. "I know I'm right."

Before Rommy could call Alice's name, she appeared with Kalen and Talen. When Rommy looked at her, Alice said, "What? I'd have to be deaf not to hear the crazy fairy." She jerked her thumb in Tinkerbell's direction.

Tinkerbell narrowed her eyes at Alice but didn't say anything. Instead, she grabbed a stick and began drawing with it on the ground. In the dim light from the moon, the outline of the island began to take shape. Tinkerbell drew a large X and tapped it with her stick.

"This is where we're at," she said. Taking her stick she dragged it across the island until she stopped at a point that was almost exactly on the other side of her drawing. She made another X. "This is where Peter is. I know it."

Finn grinned. "You're right," he said. Then he smacked his forehead. "I don't know why I didn't think of that. Of course, he went back to the old hideout. Your old man smoked him out, but most of it is still intact."

Tinkerbell glowed brightly, the tarnished pewter color turning more silver. She wore a large grin across her face.

Rommy couldn't help but smile back. "You're brilliant, Tinkerbell."

The glow got brighter. "I told you I needed to come with you."

"And you were right," said Rommy.

Then she looked around at the others. "Now that we have a good idea where Pan's at, we should all get some rest. We can go over a plan in the morning."

Alice and Finn nodded in agreement.

Together they made their way to the main cave. Several of the woven sleeping sacks that Rommy remembered when Peter Pan had kidnapped her and Alice were still hanging in various places. Despite this, the place truly looked deserted.

Rommy, Finn, and Alice each chose a sleeping sack and carefully made their way inside. Nissa slipped into Finn's sack, and Rommy was surprised to find Balo hovering in hers.

"Don't get any ideas," he said. "Yours just looks the most comfortable."

Rommy hid a smile. "Of course, Balo," she said. "You are more than welcome to share with me."

Balo huffed, but Rommy noticed he curled up close to her head. Maybe he did like her after all.

Kalen and Talen found a natural shelf in the rock and gathered some leaves to make a bed.

"We will take turns standing guard," said Kalen. "I will let my sister sleep first."

Rommy looked out the sliver of opening in her sleeping sack. She could see the lavender moon, which had grown from a slim crescent to a quarter. The pastel-colored stars were already singing.

She felt a small bubble of hope in her chest. Maybe, just maybe, they would be able to do this thing. Her mind wandered to Francie. She wondered what her friend thought of Neverland so far.

She turned her head. Balo was curled into a tight ball, and she could hear his soft snores. She watched him for a moment, and when she knew he was really sleeping, she reached into her pocket and pulled out the leaves. There were three of them. The moonlight reflected silver off their crinkled surfaces. She turned them over in her hand. Tears pressed at the back of her eyes. Could one of these have saved Lobo?

Rommy heard Unilisi's voice again. "Wishes for you, but use them wisely."

She had certainly made a mess of that, hadn't she? When she had run out of the grove, her friends had started asking her questions. The one thing that had burned bright in her brain was the quest. In all the excitement of telling Finn and Alice what Unilisi had said, the leaves were forgotten.

Rommy clenched them in her hand, crushing them. Their sharp edges pressed into her hand painfully. Tears brimmed in her eyes, and she blinked rapidly. How could she have been so stupid as to forget magical wishes?

She opened her hand again. The leaves slowly unfurled back to their original shape. Two red lines were carved into her palm from where the leaves had dug into her skin.

Rommy pressed her lips together and shoved the leaves back into her pocket. She would just focus on the quest. That was the important thing, that and rescuing Francie. After all, there was nothing she could do about Lobo now. He was gone, and not even magical leaves could bring him back. A knot formed in her stomach, but she ignored it. Nobody could find out about her secret. If they could just get off this island maybe, in time, she'd forget it was her fault Lobo was dead.

Chapter 13:
Regroup

The next morning, everyone was in a much better mood. Rommy reflected that being somewhat clean and rested definitely improved her outlook.

Finn had gotten up early and caught enough fish for all of them. After reviving the dead fire, he had made them breakfast. Now, they were all gathered around to eat and plan how they would get Francie and whichever Lost Boys wanted to leave Pan.

"I think we should keep this as our hideout," said Finn. "It's close to the Mermaid Lagoon, and Pan probably won't check it out."

Rommy nodded between bites of roasted fish. "Do you really think Pan won't realize we're here?" she asked.

Finn shrugged. "Peter isn't one to look back," he said. "He's moved on from here, so it won't even enter his head that someone would do anything different."

Alice wiped her hand across her mouth. "This place still kinda gives me the creeps." Then she shrugged. "But I guess it's better than sleeping out in the open."

Rommy smiled at the little girl's pragmatism. "I don't know that we can go back to Little Owl," she said. "First off, my father might come back there. I'm sure he's still looking for me. Second, we can't trust Tiger Lily not to inform Pan we were there, and you know she'd find out if we were there for any length of time."

Tinkerbell made a hissing noise and everyone's heads swiveled in her direction. She was perched on a large boulder, rocking back and forth, her eyes closed. Feeling everyone's stare, her eyes popped open.

"What?" she demanded.

"Is...is something wrong?" asked Rommy.

"No," snapped the fairy and then closed her eyes again. She resumed her rocking.

Rommy exchanged a glance with Nissa, who only shook her head. Rommy put down her food and looked at Finn and Alice. "We need to get Francie away from Pan," she said, "but how do we determine which Lost Boys want to go or stay?"

Finn leaned forward. "I'm glad you brought that up," he said. "I think we need to give them a choice. Just explain what's going on and then let them decide. We can't force them; it has to be their decision."

"How you gonna do that?" asked Alice. "I don't think ole Pan is going to let you stand up and make a fancy speech."

"Alice is right," said Rommy. "I agree that they should be told what's going to happen and be allowed to choose, but how will you do that?"

Finn grinned. "It's simple," he said. "We lure Pan away from the group."

Rommy snorted. "Simple, yes, but not easy," she said. "How do you propose we do that?"

"That's where you come in," said Finn. "Pan is obsessed with you, and if he thinks he can get you, he'll be stupid."

Rommy raised both her eyebrows.

Finn winked. "What? You said you didn't want to be tucked away anymore. Plus, we have to get Pan away from the Lost Boys. And I have to be the one to talk to them. If we get Francie, Pan will be hoppin' mad. He'll be ready to come after you to get her back, and if he thinks he can get you too, it will be too much for him to resist." He paused. "But you have to be sure you don't get caught or all this will be for nothing."

"We will protect Rommy," said Talen. Kalen simply nodded his agreement. "Pan can think he has Rommy and her friend alone, but we will be there too. He won't hurt either of them. This we swear." Both Talen and Kalen placed their tiny fists over their hearts and thumped their spears on the rock on which they were perched.

Rommy glanced over at Tinkerbell and then back at Finn. "Tinkerbell can come with me," said Finn. "I'm sure there are a few of the Lost Boys that will remember her and be happy to see her."

"No," said Tinkerbell, her eyes still closed.

Everyone looked at her.

"No," she repeated. After a moment, her eyes opened, and she stood up. "I will come with Rommy to lure Pan away."

Rommy grimaced. "I'm not sure that is the best..."

"I'm coming with you." Tinkerbell's voice started to climb.

"Okay, okay," said Rommy, trying to head off another outburst. "You can come with me, but you have to agree to the plan. No doing your own thing."

Tinkerbell looked offended. "I may be crazy, but I am not stupid," she said lifting her chin.

"Okay, then," said Rommy. "We get Francie, and then she and I will lure Pan away so you can talk to the Lost Boys."

"How we goin' to do that?" asked Alice, scrunching up her face. "Won't yer friend be smack in the middle of Pan and his pals? We can't just mosey on in and say come with me."

"No, we'll have to be more sneaky than that," said Rommy, laughing. "But if Francie knows we're there, she'll play along with whatever we come up with. She's sharp." Rommy grinned. "In fact, Pan might find out he bit off more than he can chew by taking Francie. She does have half a dozen brothers, after all."

Finn placed his chin in his hands. "It's still pretty early," he said. "Usually, Pan and the boys aren't up much before noon. If we can get over there soon, maybe we get Francie out before they really know what's happening. If all else fails, you'll just have to snatch her and run. That will play into our plan, anyway."

Rommy pushed to her feet. "Well, we might as well get started. If all goes well, we can get the key turned at sunrise tomorrow and be back home the next day." She paused and looked at Finn. "You are coming with us, to London, I mean?" Finn stood up, too.

"If your old man doesn't hang me by my toes from the highest mast, I will," he said, wrinkling his nose. Rommy smiled up at him, not wanting to admit how relieved she was to hear him say that. She took a deep breath and blew it out.

"Okay, then," she said, "let's go get Francie."

Chapter 14:
No Wrath Like a Fairy Scorned

The large chestnut tree was nestled in a tract of forest that surrounded a small inlet of water. It was much smaller than The Cove where Papa's shipped had been anchored, but it was still a pretty spot that provided both water to drink and fish to eat. It also provided a lot more cover than the Salt Marshes had.

Rommy, Alice, Balo, and Tinkerbell were crouched behind a cluster of trees. Tinkerbell narrowed her eyes and pointed at a large stump. It was about half a dozen yards from the chestnut tree where Pan, the Lost Boys, and Francie were supposedly camped out.

Rommy raised an eyebrow at Tinkerbell. The fairy grimaced. "That's the entrance," she said.

Finn, who was hiding behind a large beech tree with Nissa, Talen, and Kalen, nodded his head. "That's the back door," he said, his voice low. "There's a slide inside there that shoots you right into the hideout."

"Well, we can't just shoot into the hideout without a way to get out again," said Rommy, her voice rising in her frustration.

Balo clapped a small hand on her mouth. "Just announce our arrival, why don't you?" he hissed at her. Rommy glared at him until he took his hand away.

Finn pointed a finger toward the branches. Rommy squinted into the foliage, and after a moment made out a leg hanging down. The longer she looked, the more legs and arms she could see tucked into the branches. Toward the very top of the tree, in the vee of a main branch, she spotted black curls. A smile spread over her face. She slid out from behind the tree, nodding her head toward Francie. Tinkerbell followed her.

Rommy waved a hand at her. "No, stay here until I get Francie," she whispered.

Tinkerbell shook her head violently. Rommy noticed the fairy's eyes had started to dilate. She didn't want the creature to start screeching and blasting magic all over, announcing their presence to everyone.

She shrugged and put a finger over her lips. Tinkerbell smirked and flew after Rommy. Silently, Rommy flew over the ground and up to the top of the tree. She hovered where Francie slept, nestled into the base of a large branch. Rommy looked at her friend. Francie's eyes were closed and her breathing was even. Her black curls looked tangled and a bit matted, and there was a smudge of dark blue on the side of her temple. A braided length of vine was tied around one of Francie's ankles. It drooped off into the leaves below. Despite Francie's stillness, the vine periodically moved as if it was attached to something alive.

Rommy glanced around, but she didn't see Pan anywhere in the branches. A tingle of unease slid up her spine, but she worked her way between the leaves, trying not to make them rustle. She perched next to Francie, and with one hand she covered Francie's mouth while simultaneously touching her shoulder.

Francie came up swinging, her eyes wide until they alighted on Rommy's face. A smile broke across Francie's face, and pushing Rommy's hand away, she flung her arms around her friend. The girls squeezed each other tightly.

Finally, Rommy pulled back and put a finger over her mouth. Gesturing with her hand, she motioned for Francie to follow her. Francie pointed to her ankle, where the vine was tied. Then she pointed below her and mimed someone sleeping. Rommy's eyes widened when she realized what Francie was trying to tell her—the vine was attached to someone.

Rommy carefully slipped her dagger between the vine and Francie's ankle while Francie grasped the vine further down so it didn't wiggle too much. It seemed to take forever to get through the tough fibers. She made to drop the vine, but Francie grabbed her wrist. She took the vine from Rommy and tied it around a small branch. Then she gave Rommy a big grin.

It wasn't until they both were sliding back through the branches that Rommy realized Tinkerbell wasn't with her anymore. She clenched her fists. Where had that crazy fairy gotten off to now?

She spotted the tarnished glow flitting among the branches. What was Tinkerbell doing? She was going to ruin everything if she woke up any of the Lost Boys or Pan. Rommy dared not call out to the fairy. She grimaced. She'd get Francie out of here, and then she'd go back for Tinkerbell, if she had to.

"What's wrong?" whispered Francie.

Rommy just shook her head, and grasping Francie's hand, she flew out from the branches of the tree. Balo was waiting for them.

"Where's Tinkerbell?" he asked as soon as they got close enough. He craned his neck to look behind them and let out a loud huff. "What is she doing?" He shook his head. "I would ask what's wrong with her, but I already know!" He twirled a finger around the side of his head.

Francie looked between them, her eyes wide. "Who's Tinkerbell? And is that a fairy?"

"I don't know what she's up to," said Rommy to Balo, "but I thought we'd better get Francie out of there before I worry about it." Then she turned to Francie. "I'll explain things more later, but right now, we need to get further away. Pan's more likely to catch us than Tinkerbell. In fact, I'd say, if Pan had any smarts at all, he'd stay away from her."

Balo rolled his eyes. "I think he's as crazy as she is." Whirling in the air, he gestured at Francie, who was still staring at him, wide-eyed. "Stop gaping and follow me," he said.

Francie looked at Rommy, who smiled. "He's a bit grumpy, but yes, he's a fairy and we should follow him."

"I can't wait to hear this," Francie said, shaking her head.

"Later," said Rommy. "We need to get you to someplace safer before..."

The hair on the back of Rommy's neck stood up, and she whirled to find Pan not a foot away. He smiled at her, and a shiver snaked up her spine. She felt Francie's hand tighten on hers.

"Miss me, did you?" he said.

Pulling on Francie's arm, Rommy said, "Come on. Let's get out of here."

She whirled away from Pan, and, towing Francie behind her, headed into the forest.

Pan's crowing laughter floated after them. "Am I supposed to catch you if I can?" he called. "Okay, then, ready or not, here I come."

Rommy zigged and zagged between tree trunks, trying to gain some distance from Pan but not lose him all together. She wanted to get Pan far enough away that Finn could talk to the Lost Boys without Pan overhearing and trying to stop him. She didn't know how many would listen to Finn, but she wanted to give him the chance.

"Hey!" yelled Francie as a branch full of leaves smacked her in the face.

"Sorry," said Rommy, continuing to weave between the trees and branches. She didn't let go of Francie's hand but kept dragging the other girl along behind her.

She glanced over her shoulder but didn't see Pan. She swerved around a silver-colored birch, only to almost run into him.

"Found you!" he said.

Rommy peddled backwards and shoved Francie behind her. She heard the other girl gasp but ignored it, keeping her focus on Pan.

"You're going to wish you hadn't," Rommy said, pulling her dagger from the sheath at her waist.

Pan winked at Francie. "Your friend here is always ready for a fight," he said, putting both his hands up. "Do I look like a threat to you?"

"You're about as trustworthy as a clergyman with an offering plate," Francie said, crossing her arms.

Pan let out a chuckle. "And you're always ready with a joke," he said. His eyes turned to Rommy who held her dagger at the ready. "I knew you'd come." His eyes glittered.

"I only came to get my friend," said Rommy.

He slid closer. "You just can't stay away, can you?"

Rommy shifted away from him. "I would gladly never see you again, if you'd just leave my friends alone."

Pan shook his head. "No, it's just an excuse. You know you want to join me, but you're just stubborn and don't want to admit it."

Francie blew out a laugh. "Your balmy in the crumpet, for sure," she said, tossing her curls over her shoulder.

Pan ignored her, all of his concentration on Rommy. She drifted backward again, trying to stay out of Pan's reach, but he slid closer.

His hand snaked out and grabbed her dagger arm. Rommy tried to twist away from him, but he reeled her in closer until they were nose to nose.

Pan smiled. "Why won't you listen to me?" he said, his voice soft. "Why do you want to seal all the magic away here? They need me. I rescue them." His face slid next to hers until his mouth was by her ear. "I could rescue you, too."

Rommy jerked her head away just as a shriek echoed through the forest. All of them turned toward the sound. A ball of green-tinged silver light was shooting toward them.

"Liar!" The voice was so high-pitched Rommy and Pan both winced.

Pan's grip on her arm loosened and his face lit up. "Tink? Is that you?"

"Don't. Call. Me. That," the fairy gritted out between clenched teeth. The deep red had bled up her legs and arms, and she vibrated so hard she looked blurry.

Pan let go of Rommy and held up both of his hands. "I've missed you, Tink," he said. "Where've you been all this time?" His smile looked genuine, and he didn't seem to understand the danger he was in from the tiny fairy.

Tinkerbell held up both her hands. They were glowing deep red. Taking advantage of Pan's distraction, Rommy edged away from Pan toward Francie.

Beams of light shot toward Pan. He dodged away, laughing. One left a singed mark along the side of his tunic. He looked down at it, a flicker of surprise crossing his face. "Come on now, Tink, you know you're happy to see me. I'm sure happy to see you."

Rommy grasped Francie's hand. She hesitated. Tinkerbell looked determined to kill Pan, and they needed that key. But this was a good chance for them to get away, too.

Pan, meanwhile, was trying to get closer to Tinkerbell. Rommy had to agree with Francie. He was balmy on the crumpet if he didn't realize the fairy wasn't interested in a happy re-union. More beams of light shot from the fairy's hands. This time, one found its mark. Pan yelped and clapped a hand over his upper arm.

"Hey! What's wrong with you?" he said, his voice turning sulky.

Instead of answering, Tinkerbell let out a guttural growl and rocketed toward the boy who wouldn't grow up. Rommy was afraid that he wouldn't be breathing pretty soon.

Francie tugged at her hand. "Let's get out of here," she said.

Rommy shook her head, mesmerized by the scene unfolding before her.

It wasn't until Tinkerbell was almost on top of Pan that she saw the small dagger clenched in the fairy's hand. It was aimed right at Pan's heart, and he was oblivious.

Letting go of Francie's hand, Rommy shouted, "No!" and pushed toward the two. She was too late. Tinkerbell plunged the metal object into Pan's chest. His eyes opened wide with surprise. Fortunately, Rommy's shout had surprised the fairy enough that instead of his heart, the weapon was sticking out near his shoulder.

Pan's mouth formed a circle, and he grabbed at the dagger as he slowly spiraled down toward the ground and collapsed in a crumpled heap.

The fury from a moment before drained from the small fairy. She hung limp in the air, gasping. When Rommy got closer, she saw tears running down the tiny face. Tinkerbell let out a low moan, both of her hands gripping the sides of her head.

"I killed him," she muttered over and over as she backed away.

Rommy looked back and forth between the fairy and Pan who was lying still on the ground. She couldn't let Tinkerbell disappear. There was no telling what the fairy would do or where she'd go, but Rommy had to help Pan, too. Even if he wasn't as near to death as he seemed, something would surely finish him off if she left him here unconscious. She looked between Francie, whose mouth was hanging open, and Tinker-bell.

Rommy blew out a breath. She couldn't let Tinkerbell leave with that key. She called to the fairy softly and then more sharply when Tinkerbell didn't respond. The fairy raised glassy eyes toward her.

"He's not dead, not yet," Rommy said.

The fairy shook her head, her glow dimming to a sickly greenish-gray. "I don't want him to die," she said, cocking her head, "but I don't want him to live either."

"I know," said Rommy. "He hurt you, but don't you think you've punished him enough?"

"I...I...don't know," said Tinkerbell. She slowly drifted down onto a low branch.

Turning to Francie, Rommy said, "You need to go back to Finn and the others; tell them what's happened. I need some help here." She nodded her head toward Tinkerbell, who was slumped unmoving on the branch, staring blankly at her hands.

Francie blinked at Rommy and then glanced down at Pan. "It doesn't look fatal. Can't you just leave him here?" she asked.

Rommy shook her head. "No, we really can't. He'd be help-less, and there are too many things that could finish him off." She nodded toward Pan who still had not moved. She was re-lieved to see his chest rise and fall. At least he was still breath-ing.

Francie squared her shoulders. "Okay, but I have no idea where I'm at. You're going to have to point me in the right di-rection."

Rommy came to stand next to France and pointed to a sliv-er of the cliff visible between the trees. "See that?" When Francie nodded, Rommy continued. "You need to keep going toward that piece of cliff. It'll take you in the right direction at least."

Francie took a deep breath and nodded. "I'll be back as quick as I can."

Rommy squeezed Francie's hand. "Just keep going toward that bit of cliff and after a few minutes, call for Finn. He won't let you get too far off course."

Francie gave her a grin. "You can count on me," she said, and with a last glance, she pushed off and flew off in the direction of the cliffs.

Rommy watched her for a moment before turning her attention back to the situation in front of her. Tinkerbell was still sitting on the branch and seemed almost lifeless herself. At least she wasn't running away.

Rommy turned to Pan. Now to keep him from dying.

Chapter 15:
Pan's Brush With Death

With a last glance at Tinkerbell, Rommy knelt next to Pan. His breathing seemed shallow, and all the color had leached from his face. His lashes made a dark fan on his pale cheeks. He looked incredibly young.

Rommy looked closer at the tiny weapon Tinkerbell had used. Only the handle was visible. Blood seeped out around the wound. Gingerly, Rommy reached out to touch the weapon.

"You shouldn't do that," said a dull voice. Rommy twisted around. Tinkerbell had straightened up and was regarding her with clouded eyes.

"I think I need to pull it out," Rommy said.

Tinkerbell shook her head. "I poisoned it."

'What?"

Tinkerbell shrugged. "I wanted to be sure he'd die."

"Well, you touched it. Why aren't you poisoned?"

"It's just the blade that I poisoned," said Tinkerbell. "It shouldn't be on the handle, but you never know."

Rommy looked around and pulled a leaf off a nearby plant. Carefully, using it like an oven mitt, she gripped the handle of the weapon. Drawing in a deep breath, she pulled it out. It made a slight sucking sound, and Rommy fought a gag.

Peering at the small object, Rommy realized it was actually a tiny sword. It glistened with Pan's blood and something dark. She grimaced and chucked it into the undergrowth.

Blood formed a damp circle around the hole in Pan's tunic. Pulling out her own dagger, Rommy carefully cut away the fabric. She looked around for something to clean the wound so she could get a better look at it. Her own shirt was filthy, and she knew that using something dirty could cause an infection.

Tinkerbell fluttered down with a handful of pale green leaves. She thrust them at Rommy. "Here," she said. "These are safe to use."

Rommy waved away the fairy. Then she hesitated. She looked back at Pan. His face had taken on a grey-blue tinge. Quickly, before she could change her mind, she dug one of the silver leaves out of her pocket. She glanced over her shoulder. Tinkerbell was still hovering, but her gaze was on the pale green leaves still in her hands. Rommy looked at the leaf in her own hand and then at the wound on Pan's shoulder. She wasn't sure how this worked. How did you use a leaf to make a wish? Finally, she gripped it in her hand and muttered, "I wish for Pan to be okay."

Nothing happened.

She heard a faint buzz and realized Tinkerbell was hovering next to her ear. The small fairy had her head cocked. Rommy quickly closed her hand over the leaf, hoping to hide it from the fairy's inquisitive gaze.

"It doesn't work like that," Tinkerbell said after a moment.

"I don't know what you mean," said Rommy.

Tinkerbell shook the pale green leaves at her again. "Here," she said. "Take them. You have to clean off the blood before you can get rid of the poison. Then you can use the wish leaf."

So much for hiding anything from the fairy. Fear made Rommy's scalp tingle. Tinkerbell was so unpredictable, Rommy knew it was pointless to ask her not to say anything about the wish leaves.

Sighing, Rommy reached out, took the cluster of vegetation from the fairy, and carefully cleaned around the wound. Once she was done, blood continued to leak out, but it was a small trickle. More worrisome were the dark lines that spread from the wound across Pan's pale skin. She also noted his boney chest barely moving up and down as his breath had grown more shallow, and sweat beaded across his forehead.

She looked up at Tinkerbell. "What do I do now? If the wish leaf won't work, how do I get the poison out"

Tinkerbell's eyes were flat when they met Rommy's. "The swamp leech is good for removing the poison." She shrugged. "But you'll never find one in time." She nodded at Pan, and Rommy was alarmed to see the dark lines were spreading quickly, especially the one toward his heart.

Panic welled up in her. She wanted to stop Pan, but the idea of him dying right in front of her sent a swell of sorrow through her. He had seemed invincible.

"Well, what do I do?" She rose up on her knees to get closer to the fairy. "How do I save him?"

Tinkerbell paused for so long, Rommy didn't think she was going to answer. Finally, she said, "You have to use the wish leaf, of course."

Rommy clenched her hands. "But, you just said it wouldn't work. Are you *trying* to confuse me?" She stared down at Pan. If anything, he was even paler.

"If that line gets to his heart, he'll die," said Tinkerbell. She pointed with a small finger toward the dark line that was spreading relentlessly toward the center of Pan's chest.

Frustration and panic tangled into a tight lump in Rommy's throat. "How do I use this?" She flapped the silvery leaf in the fairy's face.

Tinkerbell pointed again. "Wish leaves only work if you say exactly what you want."

At Rommy's blank look, the fairy huffed. "Put the wish leaf on the wound, and then say just what you want to happen."

Rommy gently laid the leaf onto the wound. Feeling slightly ridiculous, she said, "I wish for the poison to leave."

She waited, but nothing happened.

Tinkerbell shook her head and stomped a tiny foot. "No, no, no," she said, her voice starting climb. "Say what you want to happen exactly as you want it to happen."

Rommy stared at the leaf lying on Pan's shoulder. A tiny trickle of blood leaked from around its edges.

"I wish for the poison...in Pan's body...to leave his body...immediately," she said.

At first nothing happened, and then light began to shine through and around the leaf. As the light got brighter, the leaf got darker.

Rommy could see the dark lines receding until they disappeared under the edges of the leaf. When the last one disappeared Pan jerked and then moaned. Then, with a final brilliant pulsing glow, the leaf dissolved into tiny motes of sparkling light which drifted away.

Rommy sat back on her heels, trying to absorb what just happened. Finally, she leaned forward to inspect the wound. It was still there, but the dark lines had completely disappeared. A prickling sensation made her lift her eyes, and she found Pan's brown ones regarding her. He was still pale but had lost the gray tinge. They blinked at each other.

"How are..."

"You saved..."

They both spoke at once and then stopped. Pan nodded at her.

"How are you feeling?" Rommy asked.

Pan moved his head from side to side and then closed his eyes. "Dizzy," he said. "The earth is going 'round in circles."

Rommy laid a hand on his shoulder, careful not to touch his wound which was still seeping blood. "Don't try to move just yet," she said.

Pan's eyes blinked open again. A half smile tugged at his mouth. "I...I don't think I can...even if I wanted to." His eyes fluttered shut again.

A crashing sound made Rommy snap her head around.

Through the trees, she could see Francie. Behind her were Finn, Alice, and the other fairies. She let out a long breath. Help had arrived.

Chapter 16:
To Stay or Not to Stay

Rommy watched Francie lead the others closer and was startled when she felt a hand touching hers. She looked down, and Pan's brown eyes were staring up at her.

"Don't leave me," he said, his voice hoarse.

"Don't worry," she said. "I won't leave until I know you'll be okay."

His hand tightened on hers until it was almost painful. "Don't leave me here," he said again.

Suddenly, she realized he might mean more than this current moment. She gently pulled her hand away. Standing, she faced her friends and the four Lost Boys clustered behind Finn.

She opened her mouth to explain what had happened, but suddenly Tinkerbell was in front of her, holding her glowing hands out at the advancing group.

"Uh-oh," said Alice, eyeing the fairy. "I thought she was on our side."

"I won't let you hurt him," said Tinkerbell. Her voice sounded wobbly, and her arms shook.

Francie snorted. "That's rich," she said, putting a hand on her hip. "She's the one that almost killed him, and now she's ready to blast us if we come near him. Are you crazy?"

Tinkerbell nodded solemnly. "Yes."

Francie's mouth opened and then shut.

Nobody said anything.

After a long moment, Finn stepped into the awkward silence. "It's okay, Tinkerbell," he said. "We're not here to hurt anyone. We just came to get Rommy." He smiled at the fairy. "And maybe that key?"

The fairy trembled. Then she lowered her arms. Slumping back onto the twig, she dug into the bag at her waist. She drew the green key out and held it on her lap as if it was too heavy for her to lift.

Rommy held out her hand. "I'll take it, if you'd like," she said.

Tinkerbell looked up. Her eyes had faded from the deep navy they normally were to a sea blue. Her glow was dimmer and even more green. Alarmed by the small creature's appearance, Rommy dropped her hand and leaned closer.

"Are you okay?" she asked the fairy. "You...you don't look well at all."

Tinkerbell shrugged, her movement listless. A panicky feeling unfurled in Rommy's stomach. Had the fairy accidentally ingested some of the poison meant for Pan? Her eyes met Finn's. He raised both eyebrows. It didn't seem like he knew what was wrong, either.

"It's me," said Pan. Rommy turned round to see Pan leaning up on one arm. "We had a heart bond, and trying to kill your heart bond hurts you, too." He paused and looked at Tinkerbell, his face sad. "It can kill you. You have to hate someone an awful lot to risk it."

The small fairy sniffled and refused to look up from her hands which were resting on the key. A breeze rustled the leaves, but nobody moved. Finally, Finn stepped up and gently took it from her.

"Thanks, Tinkerbell," he said. He turned and started walking away. When he realized Rommy was not following, he looked back. "Aren't you coming?"

Rommy looked from Tinkerbell to Peter Pan. He had collapsed back onto the ground, unable to hold himself up any longer. Guilt sent out wispy tendrils that squeezed her heart. The leaf should have removed the poison, but what if Pan still died? She couldn't be responsible for anyone else's death, not if she could do something.

She spread her arms out. "I can't," she said. "They both need my help. I can't just leave them here. Who knows what horrible thing might try to eat them."

"Rommy, are you crazy?" said Francie, tossing her curls over her shoulder. "I know you feel sorry for him, but you can't stay here." She turned to Finn and placed a hand on his arm, rolling her eyes. "Rommy has a bad habit of feeling sorry for people who don't deserve it. Back at school, Primrose Beechwood made her life miserable, but what does Rommy do? She feels sorry for the girl, and the last thing that prig needed was anyone's sympathy."

Rommy felt a snap of temper, and she lifted her chin. "Well, what would you have me do, Frances Hyde? You haven't been here very long, but let me tell you, everything around here can kill you, including the plants."

Francie made a face and quickly stepped away from the tree trunk she had been standing next to. Alice snorted a laugh, and Francie glared at her.

Alice moved over to Rommy and looked down at Pan. "He don't look like he's playing," she said. She poked at him with her foot. He grunted and cracked an eye. She edged away. "He looks awful." The little girl turned to look at Finn. "Maybe we should haul him out of here and back to his ole tree hideout."

Finn nodded his head. "That's a good idea, Alice," he said. He winked at Rommy. "As much as I don't want to admit it, I'd hate to see Peter eaten by something too."

A wheezy chuckle came from the boy lying on the ground. "That's...truly touching, Finn."

Finn rolled his eyes. "I'll carry his front half if you girls grab his feet."

Francie wrinkled her nose. "I still don't think he deserves any help, but if it will get you out of here..." She stepped over and gingerly picked up one leg.

Alice pushed up next to Rommy. "I'll help you, Rommy," she said, pointedly ignoring Francie.

"You can go ahead, Alice, and help us with anything that needs to be moved," said Finn.

Together the three of them hoisted Pan up and, with Alice leading the way, started toward his hideout. It was a long, slow walk through the forest. Once they got there, Rommy twisted to look at Finn, at a loss as to how they'd get Pan inside. Surely, they couldn't just shove him into the tree stump and let him shoot into the hideout.

Finn directed Alice to the tree and within a moment her hand had found a knot in the wood. At Finn's instructions she pushed, and after a moment, part of the tree trunk scrolled back, revealing an opening. Alice went through, and then Finn backed through after, with Rommy and Francie following, still holding Pan's feet.

The inside of the tree hideout was much bigger than it looked from the outside. Rommy squinted in the dimness and saw a large circular living area. Off this main living area, small openings led to alcoves. Each held a nest of sorts that served as beds. Finn made his way to one of the bigger ones. He laid Pan's top half into the opening and then supported his body while Rommy and Francie tucked his legs inside.

Alice, watching the proceedings, dusted her hands together. "There ya go," she said. "It's more than you deserve, so I hope you 'member we done ya a good turn."

Pan moaned a bit before answering. "Sure, Lost Girl," he said. "I'll remember."

Rommy turned to go, but he grabbed her hand again. "Don't leave me," he pleaded. His nut-brown eyes were large and held the sheen of tears.

Rommy felt a pang of guilt rush through her. He was all alone, and by the looks of it could barely sit up. She had no idea where the other Lost Boys had gone or when they'd be back.

She smiled at him. "We won't leave you alone until you're better," she said.

Finn's face tightened and his hands balled into fists.

Seeing his reaction, Rommy shook her hand free and stepped toward the entrance. Tipping her head, she said, "Let's go outside."

Without a word Finn, Francie, and Alice followed her outside the tree to where the others were waiting. Finn hit the knot again and waited until the door slid back into place so the tree once again looked solid.

Then he crossed his arms. "What do you mean we aren't leaving him alone?" he said.

"He almost died only a few minutes ago," said Rommy. "It would be cruel to leave him here all alone when he can barely move." She looked around at the surrounding forest. "Where are the other Lost Boys, anyway? Shouldn't they be here?"

Finn shrugged. "Who knows where they've gotten off to. Everyone tends to scatter unless Pan has some scheme or other."

"Well, we can't just leave Pan here. He's really sick." She paused and swallowed. "I think Tinkerbell really did almost kill him."

Finn threw up his hands. "We brought him to his hideout," he said. "He'll be fine. Pan's too mean to die, anyway. And the boys will be back by nightfall at the very latest."

"But he needs somebody now," said Rommy, lifting her chin.

Finn took her hand and dragged her away from the others and lowered his voice.

"We can't keep everyone here," said Finn. "If the other Lost Boys come back and Pan perks up, what then?" He shook his head. "It's too risky."

Rommy opened her mouth, but he held up a hand. "The Lost Boys that's left, well, they want to go home, but they're scared. They won't leave without me, and it would be stupid to leave any of them here for Pan to talk back around. So, what, are you going to have your friend Francie or maybe Alice stay here with him?"

Rommy crossed her arms. "Don't be ridiculous," she said. "I can stay with him."

Finn opened his mouth, shut it, and then let out a loud groan. He spun away from her and started pacing back and forth. "He's looking for a way to keep you here. Why would you make it easy for him?"

Rommy grabbed his arm, and he stopped and looked down at her.

"I'm not an idiot, Finn, no matter what you think. I don't want to put myself in danger either. But he's still weak from whatever poison Tinkerbell used," she said. "If we leave him here and he dies," she paused, "I just couldn't live with myself."

She met his gaze, and the temptation to tell him her secret was almost irresistible. If only he knew maybe then he'd understand why she couldn't risk Pan dying. She bit her lip. His gray eyes were searching her face with a mixture of concern and exasperation. No, she couldn't. What if he couldn't forgive her?

Finn blew out a breath "He could be playing you, Rommy," he said. "He's slicker than a singing eel."

Rommy shook her head. "I don't think so. You didn't see him." She shuddered. "Those black lines were so close to his heart."

Finn ran his hands through his hair until it was standing on end. "I can't make you go, and I can see your mind's made up," he said. "But promise me you'll be careful. The first time he starts to look the least bit better, hightail it out of here."

Rommy nodded. "I will, I promise," she said. She put her hand on his arm. "Thanks for understanding."

He shook her hand off his arm and shrugged. "I still think it's a mistake, but there's no budging you." He shook his head again. "Whoever said you ain't like your old man is blind as a bat. You're both a match when it comes to stubborn, that's for sure."

His words stung. Rommy was silent for a long moment before she finally said in a quiet voice, "Why don't you take everyone back to the camp then? I'll just stay long enough to make sure he's not going to die." She lifted her chin. "After all, if I wanted to kill him, I could have taken those berries Unilisi offered me."

Finn sighed. "I just don't want anything to happen to you," he said. "We're almost out of this place."

Rommy softened. "I know, Finn," she said, "and I'll be careful."

He gave one quick nod. "Okay," he said, "but if you're not back before sunset, I'm coming back for you. I don't care if Pan is still half-dead."

He turned toward the group who had been watching them.

Seeing their conversation was apparently over, Francie separated herself from the others and bounded over. She looked between the two of them and laid a hand on Finn's arm. "So, what's the plan?" she asked and wrinkled her nose. "You aren't letting Rommy play nursemaid to the crazy boy, are you?"

Rommy felt a spurt of annoyance. "*Nobody* is letting me do anything. *I* decided I'll stay back with Pan—just until he's better—and Finn will take the rest of you back to camp."

Francie blinked at Rommy's sharp tone. "O...kay then," she said. Pressing her lips together, Francie tightened her hand on Finn's arm and pulled him toward the others. "I guess we have our orders."

Rommy felt a knot in her stomach as she watched them walk away. She didn't know why Francie was suddenly getting on her nerves, but she could tell she'd hurt her friend's feelings just now. She sighed. Another thing she had messed up, but she didn't have time to worry about it now, though.

Suddenly, she frowned and looked around. "Where is Tinkerbell?"

Balo, who had been hovering nearby, buzzed closer. "She flew off somewhere," he said, flapping a hand. "And good riddance, I say. We have the key. We don't need the crazy fairy, too."

Rommy felt guilty for the relief that flooded through her. While she hoped the little fairy was okay, she couldn't help but be glad that Tinkerbell couldn't tell anyone about those leaves.

Chapter 17:
Everybody's Got a Story

When Rommy returned to Pan, his eyes were closed. He appeared to be asleep, so she started looking around until she found a small pail. However, when she started to leave to fill it with water, his eyes popped open.

"Where are you going?" he asked.

Rommy turned in surprise. "I think you need some water," she said. "I was going to go find some for you."

His eyelids drooped, and he mumbled, "Water's good."

She left the tree and found a small pool of water not too far from the chestnut. After peering into the water for any sorts of creatures—the memory of the water nixie made her shudder—she dipped the pail in and filled it to the top.

Once she was back inside, she looked around. There was a basket of some kind of fruit and various types of roots so she wasn't too worried about what Pan would eat. Now that he had water, Rommy decided she'd just stay for an hour or so to make sure he wasn't suffering any permanent effects from the poison. She sat on a big cushion made of some kind of moss and leaned back against the inside of the tree trunk. She felt her own eyes getting heavy.

The sound of her name jolted her back to wakefulness. She could see one leg hanging out of the alcove where Pan had been resting. She blinked the sleep out of her eyes and pushed to her feet. She walked toward him warily. She didn't know how long she'd been asleep, and she wouldn't put it past Pan to try to trick her.

She needn't have worried. Although he was sitting up, his slumped posture told her he was still weak. He looked up at her, relief spreading over his face.

"You're still here," he said. "I thought you had left, too."

She gave a half smile. "No, I just dozed off, I guess," she said. She stopped close enough to see him but far enough away that he couldn't reach her. "Did you need something? I can get you some fruit or some water."

Pan shook his head and looked at her from half-lidded eyes. "No, I just...I didn't want to be alone is all," he said. His words sounded a bit slurred, and his face looked flushed.

Rommy moved forward and gingerly put a hand on his forehead. It was hot. Now what was she going to do? He must have seen the alarm on her face because he smiled. "You're worried about me," he said, rolling his head toward her. "I knew you cared." His eyes started to drift shut. She hurried to get him some water.

When she got back, she shook his shoulder until he opened his eyes again. She put the cup to his lips until he took a drink, some of the water dribbling down the front of his tunic.

"I think you've got a fever," she said. "You need to drink water." She hid the panic bubbling up. She had no idea what to do for a fever on this stupid island. Back home, she could have given him some birch bark tea and someone could call a doctor. But here—she had no idea. Suddenly, she wished she had just gone with the others and didn't have to deal with another problem.

Pan reached out and grasped her hand with his hot one. She flinched, but he held on. "It's not a fever," he said. "I shouldn't tell you because you'll leave." He let out a rusty-sounding laugh, not at all like his usual high-pitched one. "It's the the effects of the poison leaving. I'll be okay in the morning." He looked up at her. "Thanks to you," he said. He squeezed her hand. "You're the one that took out the poison, weren't you?"

Rommy gently tugged her hand away and nodded. "Just because I don't want to join your band of Lost Boys doesn't mean I want you die," she said. Unsure what to do, she began to move briskly around the interior, tidying things up. There were pieces of clothing, sticks, and other items strewn throughout the living spaces and hanging out of the alcoves.

A dreamy smile crossed Pan's face. "She used to do that," he said. "But she'd always sing or hum while she worked." He turned his eyes up to hers.

"Who was she?" asked Rommy.

He gave a long sigh but instead of answering the question, he said, "I thought she was happy." His mouth turned down. "And then she left."

Shaking his head, he stared down at his hands. Then he looked up and gave a hopeful smile. "Do you sing?"

Rommy let out a half laugh. "Not hardly," she said. "At least not so anyone would want to listen."

"That's right," he said. "You don't sing; you fight."

She slid a glance at him from the corner of her eye and shrugged. "We all have our talents, I suppose—even you. "

"Not according to my Da," said Pan. "He always told me I wasn't good for nothing but costing money to feed."

Rommy drew in a sharp breath. "But surely your father didn't mean it," she said.

Pan cackled, his laugh sounding more like his normal crow. "Oh, he meant it, all right, and I had the bruises to prove it."

Rommy frowned. Not knowing what to say in answer to that, she turned away to pick up some clothing that was hanging from an alcove. It was dirty but she folded it anyway and tucked it into the space.

Pan shrugged. "It's why he left, I suppose, but he must have been right because everyone leaves me...eventually."

Rommy continued her tidying as she gathered her thoughts. Despite how awful he'd been, Rommy felt an ache in her chest when she thought of a young boy being told he was worthless and being mistreated and finally abandoned. Was it any wonder he was twisted on the inside?

Finally, she turned to face him. "That's not completely true," she said. "You have your Lost Boys, this island. You've found a place to belong here."

Pan stared down at his hands. "Nah, I haven't found a place," he said. "I've made a place. I've made a family, but some of 'em, they don't know they're better off here. They don't want to stay. Even Finn left." He looked up at her, and his mouth curved into a sly smile. "But I can't say that I blame him."

Rommy felt heat crawl up her neck, and she cleared her throat. Ignoring his last comment, she continued with her task.

"Maybe if you asked people instead of making them, they'd be more inclined to stay with you."

Pan's eyes narrowed. "I asked you," he said.

Rommy sighed. "But I don't belong here...Peter," she said. "You and I both know that." Even though she knew it was the truth, she couldn't help the prick of guilt his words caused, and she returned to her tidying, not wanting him to see her feelings which were probably clearly written on her face.

"But you want me to be alone forever," he said. He tossed his head to get the hair out of his eyes. "You want to seal me away here, and I'll never have any more family."

The guilt reached up and choked her. Maybe he had made some mistakes, but look what she had done. If everyone knew, would they want to seal her here forever, too? She swallowed past the lump in her throat. All she wanted was to leave. She glanced at him over her shoulder. Her eyes narrowed as she looked at him more carefully. His posture was straighter, and his face had returned to a normal color. She also noticed his movements seemed sharper, less sluggish.

Dusting her hands together, she gave a half smile. "You seem to be doing better," she said. She pointed to the pail. "You've got water and food. I should probably be going."

Pan let out a long sigh. "I knew you were going to say that." He swung his legs down. Rommy didn't wait but moved toward the door. She glanced over her shoulder. Pan hadn't moved but his eyes followed her.

"Goodbye, Peter," she said and walked through the door. The last thing she saw was Pan put his chin in his hands, a frown on his face. She hurriedly pushed the knot and the bark slid back into place. Then she leaped into the air. If she flew fast enough, maybe she'd get away, not just from Pan, but from the guilt.

Chapter 18:
To Do or Not to Do

Rommy wove her way through the trunks of beeches, birches, and chestnuts that hugged the forested coastline where Pan's hideout was located. Once she cleared the trees, she flew over the grasslands.

But no matter how fast she flew, she couldn't forget Peter Pan's face when she hurried out the door. He was crazy and mean and scary.

But he'd had a life before Neverland, and it sounded like it hadn't been a very nice one. The people in it—his father—had been truly awful. Rommy blinked back the tears that suddenly threatened. Papa had yelled at her and hurt her feelings, but she knew, deep down, he loved her. Papa might have lost his way a bit since her younger brother was killed, but Peter's father—he sounded hateful and mean. She swiped a hand across her eyes.

Ahead lay the river and the willow where she and Alice had found shelter, at least for a little while, what seemed like a lifetime ago. She alighted on one of the branches and sat to catch her breath. She stared down at the water flowing below.

She had been so certain what they needed to do—stop Pan. But now, she had seen past Pan to the boy Peter, and the idea of sealing that boy on this island forever made her stomach clench.

They had to stop Pan, but at what cost to the boy, Peter? After all, everyone made mistakes. Look at what she had done, and she didn't even have the excuse that Peter did. Suddenly, things weren't as clear as they had been that morning.

Rommy wished she could go back to before she had seen the lost, abandoned boy under Pan's layer of crazy. She let out a long sigh.

The sun was no longer high in the sky. It had to be afternoon. Rommy stood up. The last thing she wanted to do was spend the night alone anywhere on this island. The thought sent another tendril of guilt. If they succeeded, Pan would spend the rest of his nights mostly alone here.

Rommy pushed off the branch into the sky. As she sped toward her friends, her mind churned. They had to stop Pan, but was sealing him here forever really the answer?

Maybe Finn would have some insights. At that thought, she put on another burst of speed, but no matter how fast she flew, the question wouldn't leave her alone.

Chapter 19:
The Green-Eyed Monster

I t was with a sigh of relief that Rommy heard the sound of the waterfall. Within a few moments, it came into view. As she flew around the last bend in the river, she came to a halt mid-air.

Standing off by themselves near the waterfall were Finn and Francie. He was leaning in close to her, and she had her face tipped up to his.

Cold iced over Rommy's skin, and a hot feeling unfurled in her stomach. She wrapped her arms around her middle. She must have made some kind of sound because the two jerked apart and whirled toward her.

She forced herself to straighten and smiled. "Hey, I'm back," she said.

Finn backed further from Francie. "She, uh, had this thing in her eye," he said, but Rommy noticed he wouldn't meet her gaze, and color had crept into his cheeks.

Francie was oblivious to any tension. "Never mind about my eye," she said. A grin lit up her face, and she ran toward Rommy. Francie threw her arms around Rommy. "I'm so glad you're here and safe," she said. "I still can't believe you stayed back with that Peter Pan. My brothers are idiots sometimes, but he's truly balmy on the crumpet."

Rommy nodded, but her eyes followed Finn who still wouldn't look at her. She pulled away from Francie.

"Yes, he's got some problems, that's for sure." Francie made to link her arm in Rommy's, but Rommy evaded her and walked quickly toward the others. Alice was playing some kind of game with Walter, the youngest Lost Boy, and Nissa was darting in and out. The little girl's laughter rang out like a chime, and Walter had a big grin on his face. Alice motioned to a slight boy who was hanging back. Rommy remembered him from her time in Pan's camp, but his name escaped her.

On a nearby rock, a boy with brown hair and big dark eyes was feeding something to a squirrel perched on his shoulder. He pointedly ignored a redheaded boy hopping up and down in front of him. She smiled. She certainly remembered Henry, the redhead, and she thought the other boy's name was George. Unless they were in the caves, it seemed like the older Lost Boys had elected to stay in Neverland. She wondered where they had been while she'd been with Peter.

When Rommy entered the circle of stones around the fire pit, all the others stopped what they were doing and looked up at her. She swallowed. What would they say when she voiced her doubts? *Should* she voice her doubts?

She cleared her throat. "Well, when I left, Peter seemed to be okay," she said and then shrugged. "Tinkerbell didn't kill him." Glancing around, she continued, "Speaking of Tinkerbell, does anyone know where she went?"

Finn shook his head. "When we were moving Pan, she took off. Nobody's seen her since," he said.

Alice perched on the edge of one of the rocks. "So's have you figured out how we're going to get past them mermaids to that sighing cave?"

Francie scrunched up her face. "Mermaids? You have to be joking." She looked at Finn. "She's making that up, right?"

Finn shook his head.

Alice rolled her eyes. "You'd think you flitten' through the sky and fairies buzzing around would make mermaids kinda believable."

Francie frowned at the little girl. "Well, excuse me," she said. "It's not like I'm used to all this...this craziness."

Rommy held up her hands. "Crazy or not, Alice is telling the truth, Francie. We have to swim down to the Cave of Sighs to turn the key in the lock and that will start closing the passage between Neverland and our world. We'll have from sunrise to sunrise to get out. Anyone still here won't ever be able to leave." She looked at Alice. "And this place does take a bit of getting used to."

Alice softened a bit. "Yeah, and the thing ya gotta remember is just about everything here can kill you. Some of the creatures are downright helpful, but they could still kill ya, if they wanted to."

Francie stepped closer to Finn and leaned against his arm. Rommy noticed he didn't move away. That feeling in her stomach flared again, and she dropped her eyes.

Walter's voice brought her back to the present. "How're you gonna get past them mermaids?" He scrunched up his face. "How can anyone hold their breath that long?"

Rommy sighed and plopped down on the sandy ground. "I don't know that yet, Walter," she said. She looked at the fairies.

"Do you know of any way to magically extend how long we can stay underwater? I don't know that we have any chance against the mermaids otherwise."

Balo tapped a finger against his mouth. "I've heard there's a plant that can make you breathe underwater," he said. Then he threw up his hands. "But I don't know what it is or where to find it. It's impossible." He shook his head. "Whoever goes down there may as well plan on dying."

Francie's eyes got big, but Rommy just rolled hers. She was used to Balo's negativity.

"Maybe Little Owl will know," she said.

Finn looked at her from across the fire, but she refused to meet his eyes. "We should go ask her sooner rather than later," he said. "Not only is Pan weak at the moment, which gives us some breathing room, but the sooner we turn that key, the sooner we can all get out of here."

Again, Peter Pan's face flashed through her mind as he told her that everyone in his life had left him. She swallowed down the guilt that kept forming a lump in her throat.

"I don't think Peter will be bothering us for a while yet," she said. "There's no need to rush into things. We want to be sure we're doing the right thing."

Finn crossed his arms, and his eyes narrowed. "So, it's Peter now?"

Rommy jerked her head up and for the first time since she had returned their eyes met. "What's that supposed to mean?"

"It means, I'm wondering what ole Pan told you since this is the second time now that you've called him Peter. You've always called him Pan before," said Finn. "And since when do you want to slow this quest down? This morning you were as eager to get shod of this place as any of us." He nodded around the circle.

Francie put her hand on Finn's arm and squeezed. Rommy saw it but pulled her gaze away. She jutted out her chin.

"I don't think it's wrong to make sure we're doing the right thing when this is permanent," she said. "I haven't forgotten that we have to stop Peter...Pan, but he's a person, too. I mean, we all make mistakes." She faltered, the memory of Lobo rising up in her mind. "I just think...well...that maybe we have to understand why he does the things he does." She shrugged. "I mean, what if we can help him?"

Finn's face softened, and he started to speak, but Francie cut him off. "How can you even think about wanting to help him? After everything I've heard about him, it sounds like he deserves what he gets," she said, her voice loud. "The problem with you, Rommy, is you always feel so sorry for everyone." Francie put her hands on her hips. "You need to be smarter than to fall for whatever sob story he told you." She twisted back toward Finn. "Tell her, Finn. Tell her she's letting that soft heart of hers get in the way."

Rommy felt like she'd been slapped. "I'm not falling for some sob story, as you put it," she said. "What I'm saying is what we are going to do is permanent. It's not only that it can't be stopped once it's started, but it can never be undone. Ever. Shouldn't we be sure he's beyond help before we lock him away here forever?"

Francie snorted. "It sounds like that's exactly what he deserves," she said. "I mean, he kidnapped a bunch of little kids, and from what I've seen, he's not too nice to them, either. And he certainly wasn't nice to me. He deserves to pay for his mistakes, if you ask me."

Finn stepped forward and put one hand on Francie's shoulder and held the other one out to Rommy. "Francie's right..." he started.

"Of course she is," muttered Rommy. She felt ridiculously close to tears, and the last thing she wanted to do was to start crying in front of everyone. She scrambled to her feet. "I...I...I need to go wash up," she said and turned away from the group. She walked toward the pool at the base of the waterfall. She hadn't gone more than a few steps when a small hand slipped into hers.

"I know she's yer friend, but that Francie sure has a lot to say," said Alice.

Rommy gave a watery smile. "That's just Francie's way," she said. "She means well, but sometimes, she can be..."

"Bossy? A know-it-all?" Alice said, lifting an eyebrow.

A small laugh escaped Rommy's mouth. "You could say that," she said.

"But she does have a point." Alice held up her hands. "I'm on your side, but you have to admit, you've kinda gone and done an about-face. What did Pan say to you?"

Rommy bit her lip. "Look, I know he has to be stopped. I didn't suddenly lose all my reason, even though you all probably think that," she said. "It's just his father told him he was worthless and then just abandoned him. And...and...doesn't everyone deserve a second chance, even if they make a really big mistake?"

Alice whistled. "Well, I'd say he's done more than make a mistake. But havin' a pop like that'd mess a person up," she said.

"Some of them street kids I ran with, they had pops that were nasty pieces of work. It can send you 'round the bend."

"That's what I mean," said Rommy. "I'm not saying we shouldn't close the passage, but knowing what I know, it's not as easy to do. Before, Pan was just the enemy."

Alice squeezed her hand. The two of them stood on the edge of the pool. Rommy pulled off her boots and rolled up her pant legs, letting her feet dangle in the cool water. Alice plopped down next to her. She bumped Rommy's shoulder with her own.

"And just so's you know, Finn ain't taken with her," she said.

Rommy whipped her head in Alice's direction, her cheeks turning pink. "What in the world does that have to do with anything?"

Alice chuckled. "I may only be six, but I gots two eyes. It's not just Pan that's got yer feathers ruffled."

Rommy crossed her arms. "I don't know what you're talking about."

Alice grinned. "Okay, whatever you say," she said. "But Francie has been batting her eyes at Finn ever since she got here." She clasped her hands under her chin and fluttered her eyelashes. "Ooh, Finn, you're so big and strong. Ooh, Finn, I needs yer help."

Rommy laughed and pushed Alice's shoulder. "Francie's just that way," she said. "She flirts with anything in pants."

"Well, I don't think Finn is too impressed, is all I'm saying."

Rommy wrinkled her nose. "I don't know," she said. "He didn't seem to mind."

"Ha!" said Alice. "I knew you two was sweet on each other."

Her face red, Rommy waved a hand. "We're friends, Alice, but all that doesn't really matter. I don't know what to do now." She gestured back toward the campfire. "And everyone is looking at me to say what we're going to do next." She shook her head and put her face in her hands. "And I just don't know anymore."

Alice put a small hand on her back. "Maybe you should talk to Little Owl," she said. "She always knows what to do."

Rommy lifted her head and threw her arms around Alice. "Alice, you're a genius," she said. "That's just what I'm going to do."

"Well, this genius needs to breathe," came Alice's muffled reply. "Do ya mind?"

Rommy let her go. "Tell the others where I'm going so they don't worry, but wait until I'm gone."

Alice frowned. "Do you think it's a good idea to go alone?"

Rommy looked at the sky. The sun was low, but it wasn't twilight yet. "I have enough time to get there before it's dark," she said. "I have to talk to Little Owl alone."

Alice nodded reluctantly. "Okay, I guess," she said. Then she grabbed Rommy's hand and squeezed. "But promise you'll be real careful."

Rommy smiled. "Of course, I will." Without waiting, she jumped up and stuck her wet feet back into her boots and lifted into the air. Little Owl would know what to do.

Chapter 20:
When You Need a Little Advice

Rommy landed back behind the cluster of homes at the small village. The problem was that they all looked so much alike she had a hard time telling them apart. For a moment, she wished she'd let Alice come along, but then she shook her head. No, she needed to talk to Little Owl on her own. Narrowing her eyes, she counted the round tents, trying to determine which one belonged to the older woman.

While she didn't think Chief Hawk Eye would mind her visiting, the last thing she wanted to do was run into Tiger Lily.

"What are you doing here, lurking behind my grandmother's home?"

Rommy jumped. It was as if her thoughts had conjured the other girl.

Tiger Lily stood tall, her thick black braid over one shoulder, and a long polished stick in her hand.

"I want to talk to Little Owl," said Rommy, straightening her shoulders.

Tiger Lily tossed her braid over her shoulder. "You could come around the front, you know," she said. "Father likes you. Why, I don't know."

Rommy gritted her teeth but ignored the comment. "I didn't want to disturb anyone," she said.

Tiger Lily lifted one shoulder. "Grandmother isn't here. She's out gathering plants."

"Well, do you know when she'll be back?"

Again, the girl lifted a shoulder. "When she goes off to gather plants, she can be gone a long time."

The air went out of Rommy, and her shoulders slumped. She had counted on Little Owl helping her decide what to do. She dreaded going back to Finn and the others with her mind still uneasy.

"I don't suppose it will bother anyone if you wait." The words were spoken grudgingly.

Tiger Lily turned away from Rommy and began making her way back around the tents. Rommy followed her, not sure what else to do.

The older girl kept walking until she reached a small cleared space on one side of the encampment. Not a single green thing grew in the space and the dirt looked like many feet had trampled it. Circling the space were a series of wooden posts, and vines were strung among them, making a kind of fence with only a small opening through which to enter. Several sticks that looked like the one Tiger Lily held were leaning against one of the posts. Tiger Lily walked to the center of the circle, completely ignoring Rommy, who leaned against a post, watching.

Tiger Lily stood tall in the center, her stick straight up and down in front of her. She closed her eyes and took a deep breath. Then she began to move. Holding the stick with both hands in the very middle, she twirled it this way and that, lunging out and up. It reminded Rommy of a combination of fencing and dancing. She walked over to where the other sticks were and ran a hand down one. It was completely smooth.

"I will show you," said Tiger Lily, startling Rommy. "I need someone to practice with."

Rommy hefted one of the sticks in her hands. It was heavier than her fencing sword, but she was intrigued.

Tiger Lily motioned for Rommy to join her in the center of the circle. Rommy held the stick with both hands, like she'd hold a sword. Tiger Lily made a clicking noise.

"No, you need to hold it in the middle, like this." She demonstrated by putting her hands directly in the center of her own stick. Rommy copied her.

"Now, you use the two ends to strike your opponent." Tiger Lily whirled her stick and brought it down with a crack on Rommy's. The reverberation ran up Rommy's arms, making her step back.

Tiger Lily nodded. "Now you try."

Rommy experimented with moving the stick the way she had seen Tiger Lily do it. It felt awkward. She wasn't used to using two hands.

For the first time since she had met her, Tiger Lily smiled at her. "You have the touch," she said. "Now try to strike my stick."

Rommy brought her pole around and over and tapped Tiger Lily's stick. The older girl chuckled. "You will not win any matches with a tap like that. Come, you can do better. I've seen you fight."

She started to circle Rommy, moving her stick as she did. She brought it over and around, and out of instinct, Rommy blocked the older girl's strike, then swirled back and forward for her own strike which hit true.

Tiger Lily nodded her head. "Good, good," she said. "You can feel the rhythm in the wood."

Rommy wrinkled her nose. "Rhythm in the..." but before she could finish, Tiger Lily brought her pole down again, this time rapping one of Rommy's hands.

"Ouch!"

Tiger Lily laughed. "You must concentrate," she said.

As they circled each other, striking and blocking each other, Tiger Lily asked, "Why did you come to see Grandmother? I did not think you would return here for your... quest."

Rommy eyed her warily. She wasn't sure how much she should share with this girl who loved Peter Pan. "I... I think it is a good idea to make sure you are doing the right thing."

Tiger Lily lifted one eyebrow. "The right thing? I thought you had decided sealing Peter in Neverland was the right thing." She twirled and did a series of strikes that had Rommy dancing to keep up.

Once they were circling again, Rommy answered. "It seemed like it was, but..." she trailed off as she went into her own series of strikes, taking the other girl by surprise. The two danced back and forth, each trying to get in a good blow.

Tiger Lily wasn't even breathing hard. "Peter has been here a long time," she said, backing away to give Rommy time to catch her breath. "He is more of this world than yours now."

Rommy felt a spurt of surprise. She had expected the other girl to tell her she shouldn't seal Pan here. "What are you saying?" Rommy asked circling the other girl again.

"I'm saying..." Tiger Lily went on a series of strikes that had Rommy busy, trying to block each blow. One landed on her hand, making her fingers numb, and she almost dropped her pole. "Peter doesn't belong in your world anymore."

Rommy was so startled that when Tiger Lily struck again, she didn't have time to block the other girl, and her stick clattered to the ground.

"Don't look so surprised," said Tiger Lily, planting her stick in the ground next to her foot. "I have loved Peter for a long time, but he does not love me or anyone, not truly." She made a face. "You were right about that, as much as I didn't want to believe you."

Rommy jerked her head in astonishment. When she had rescued the older girl in the jungle from a killer plant, she hadn't thought Tiger Lily had heard anything she said about Pan. Still, Tiger Lily's change of heart didn't fix Rommy's dilemma.

"But he told me about his father, about how he was abandoned," said Rommy. "I just wonder if maybe we can help him instead of locking him away here forever. We all make mistakes. Shouldn't he get a second chance, too?"

Tiger Lily snorted. "Peter is not like me or you. He has become a creature of Neverland, and this is where he belongs. He doesn't fit in your world anymore. You will not be hurting him by keeping him here, and you may save others."

Rommy just stared at the older girl.

Tiger Lily shrugged. "I know you have to go into Mermaid Lagoon. There is a plant that can help you breathe underwater, and I know where to find it."

Rommy blinked at her. Tiger Lily was the last person she had expected to help her.

The other girl tapped her stick on the ground. "Are you just going to stare at me, or do you want my help?"

"Oh, yes," said Rommy. "I...that would be...that is, I wasn't sure how we were going to get past the mermaids."

"Even if you can breathe underwater, that still won't be easy. And my help doesn't come freely," said Tiger Lily. She pressed her lips together, looking away. "If I help you, you have to let me leave with you when you go."

Rommy felt the air rush out of her in a big breath. If someone had told her that when she came to see Little Owl, it would be Tiger Lily who would help her see things clearly and would offer to help them, Rommy would have laughed at the absurdity. Now the girl wanted to leave Neverland. Then, Rommy remembered Little Owl's words.

"Yes, you can come with us," said Rommy. She hesitated. "But..."

Tiger Lily narrowed her eyes. "I know I will be different from the other girls, but I do not care." She flung a hand out. "There is nothing for me here. Our people are slowly dying out. I want more than to be stuck here for the rest of my life."

Rommy nodded. "It's true," she said. "You will be different, but I think...I know you can make a place for yourself." She smirked. "I don't think even Primrose would bother you more than once."

"I don't know this Primrose, but she will be sorry she interferes with me any time," Tiger Lily said, scowling.

Rommy smothered a laugh. "Well, I guess now we both need to talk to your grandmother."

She leaned the pole back against the post, walked to where Tiger Lily stood, and held out her hand. Tiger Lily clasped it. The two girls' eyes met and understanding flowed between them. Rommy thought, not for the first time since she had arrived at Neverland, that allies came in many shapes and sizes.

Chapter 21:
Every Beginning
Starts With an Ending

When the two girls approached Little Owl's home, they heard voices. They looked at each other, and without a word both of them reached for the tent flap.

Inside, they found Finn and Alice with Little Owl who was sorting plants on a wooden table.

"But she said she was coming to talk to you." Finn was speaking. He nudged Alice. "Isn't that what she told you? It's already dark. Something must have happened to her."

Rommy stepped into the tent. "I'm fine," she said.

Finn and Alice both spun in her direction.

Little Owl smiled and nodded her head. "See, young Finn? Your worry was for nothing." Little Owl looked between Tiger Lily and Rommy, and her smile widened even more.

"I'm surprised you even noticed I hadn't come back," said Rommy, crossing her arms.

Finn frowned. "Why wouldn't I notice? Alice said you'd be back by sunset, and the sun has done set."

"I thought you might have been...distracted."

Alice rolled her eyes. "Don't be a git," she said. "We was all worried when you didn't show up." She looked at Tiger Lily and tipped her head in the older girl's direction. "Why's she here?"

Alice had reason to be suspicious of Tiger Lily after the girl had kidnapped her to try to win Pan's favor.

Rommy let a smile spread over her face. "Tiger Lily is going to help us," she said.

"Since when is she on our side?" said Alice. She crossed her arms. "If she's here, Pan ain't far behind."

Tiger Lily's eyes narrowed. "I am through with Peter," she said. Her eyes suddenly looked sad. "No matter how much I wish it, I cannot change his shape."

Little Owl's eyes were soft as she laid a hand on her granddaughter's cheek. "Ah, Granddaughter, that is a difficult lesson to learn, that we cannot change others, no matter how much we wish it...or how much we love them."

Tiger Lily blinked her eyes several times before answering. "Yes, Grandmother, Peter won't change, or rather he's changed too much to go back to what he once was." She lifted her chin a bit. "So, I have decided to leave Neverland." She turned toward Alice. "Does this answer your question about why I am 'on your side'?"

Alice lifted one shoulder. "I'll believe it when I see it," she said.

Rommy stepped forward and laid a hand on Alice's shoulder. "Tiger Lily knows of a plant that will help us breathe underwater," she said. She looked at Finn. "This is how we can get past the mermaids."

Finn lifted an eyebrow. "Get past the mermaids? So, now you've decided we're doing this quest? Are you sure you ain't gonna change your mind in another hour?"

Rommy frowned. "I never said I had changed my mind. I said I wanted to be sure, and now I am."

Finn still looked skeptical, and his gaze shifted to Tiger Lily. "How do we know she's telling the truth about this here plant?"

Tiger Lily took a step forward, her hand going to the knife at her waist. "I do not lie," she said. "Nobody questions my honor."

Little Owl laid a hand on her granddaughter's arm. "Now, now, it is not easy for former enemies to learn trust. You must show some patience."

Tiger Lily glared at Finn. "Grandmother speaks wisdom." Her eyes narrowed again. "But do not question my honor again."

Finn held up both hands. "Hey, I'm not the one who was pining after Pan," he said.

"But you did not hurry to leave him, either," the older girl shot back and then her gaze slid to Rommy. "Not until your own heart started to speak, if I'm not mistaken."

Finn's face flushed. "It wasn't for Pan that I stayed," he said stiffly. "It was for the Lost Boys."

Rommy stepped between the two and pushed them apart. "Look, when I came here, Tiger Lily was the last person I expected to help me." She cast an apologetic look at the older girl. "But we need her. Without that plant, we don't really have any chance of getting past those mermaids, and besides, she's the one that helped me see things more clearly."

Finn seemed to deflate, but Tiger Lily did not relax her stance. Rommy raised an eyebrow at her. "Tiger Lily? I trust you," she said. "That's going to have to be enough until you prove yourself to everyone else, I think."

Tiger Lily let out a puff of air, and after a moment, her shoulders relaxed. She turned to her grandmother. "I am sorry, Grandmother, but I must leave this place."

Little Owl smoothed a gnarled hand over her granddaughter's thick, black hair. Her eyes were wet. "Yes, yes you do," she said. "I will miss you, Granddaughter, but it is for the best."

Tiger Lily wiped delicately at her eyes, and Rommy moved away. She felt like she was intruding on a very private moment.

"Shouldn't we be finding this here plant?" asked Alice.

Rommy shook her head. "Give them some time," she said.

Tiger Lily straightened from her grandmother's embrace. "I do not need more time," she said. She turned to face the group. "It will take two of us. The plant grows on the cliffs at Mermaid Lagoon."

"Well, that's convenient," said Rommy. "I'll come with you."

Finn shook his head. "No, I think I should be the one to go," he said. "I know the cliffs better than you do."

Rommy crossed her arms. "Don't be ridiculous," she said. "The Lost Boys trust you, not me. It's not going to help anything if I go back and you have disappeared."

Finn sighed. "I suppose you have a point," he said.

Rommy lips curved into a half smile. "Are you actually admitting that I'm right and you're wrong for once?"

An answering smiled tipped Finn's mouth. "I wouldn't go that far," he said. He reached out and squeezed her hand.

The knot that had seemed to take up permanent residence in Rommy's stomach since their disagreement at Pan's hideout started to unravel. Maybe things between them could be like before, even with her secret. Once they got back to London, maybe it wouldn't matter as much. She shook the thought away. There were bigger things to worry about right now, but she couldn't help the foolish smile that spread across her face.

Chapter 22:
Plans, Plans, and More Plans

Little Owl moved to her rocking chair and gestured for all of them to gather around her. "You must make your plan now," she said. "Once the key is turned in the lock, time will become your enemy."

Alice, Finn, Tiger Lily, and Rommy sat at the older woman's feet. A deep sadness welled up in Rommy. She would miss Little Owl and her warmth and wisdom. While Neverland had proved both dangerous and disappointing in many ways, the woman sitting in front of her had been one of the bright spots.

"We should go at the next sunrise," said Finn, interrupting her thoughts. "The longer we delay, the more chance there is for everything to blow up in our faces."

"We won't get much sleep," said Rommy.

Finn paused, "You're right, but if we don't go at the next sunrise, that gives Pan a whole day more to recover. Not to mention, your father is still looking for you. If he finds you before you turn that key, I think we're done."

Rommy sighed. Exhaustion weighed her down, but Finn was right. She nodded. "Tiger Lily and I will go to get the plant," she said. "We can all meet on the beach right before sunrise. If...no when we turn that key, we'll need to get to Papa to persuade him."

Alice cocked her head. "I don't think them pirates is going to be happy about leaving here," she said.

Rommy shrugged. "Surely, some of them will want to go back," she said. "The rest can stay here if they like. The one we have to worry about persuading is Papa."

Tiger Lily leaned forward. "Before we worry about your father, we must get around the mermaids."

Alice shook her head. "I don't see no way around them fish girls," she said.

Tiger Lily rolled her eyes. "Then it is a good thing it is not up to you," she said. "We must distract them while one of us finds the lock."

Little Owl nodded her head. "It is important that several of you work together."

"Francie is as good of a swimmer as I am, but she doesn't really understand this place yet." Rommy took in Alice's pale face. "And Alice doesn't swim, so that leaves me, Finn, and Tiger Lily."

"And we have to have enough of the plant," said Tiger Lily. "It does not last very long."

"I think you and me can distract the three of them, don't you?" Finn looked at Tiger Lily who nodded. Then he turned his gaze to Rommy. "That leaves you to swim with the key. Do you think you can do that and get back to the beach before your air runs out?"

Rommy smiled and winked. "Those fish girls have nothing on me," she said.

Tiger Lily pushed to her feet. "It is settled then," she said. "We will get the fish weed, and then we will meet the rest at the beach."

Rommy, Finn, and Alice stood up, too. Little Owl followed them to the door. Rommy hugged the older woman tightly. "Are you sure you won't come with us?" she whispered in the older woman's ear.

Little Owl patted her back. "No, Child, but I thank you." She pulled back from Rommy and looked deep into her eyes. "You have the good and true heart of a warrior. Don't forget that, no matter where life leads you."

Rommy blinked back tears.

"I won't," she said.

Before she had stepped back fully, Alice threw her arms around Little Owl's waist. The older woman bent and kissed the top of the little girl's head. "Blessings on your journey, Little One." Alice sniffled loudly and swiped a hand across her eyes.

"I wish you was goin' with us," she said. "But you ain't got a place back in our world, do you?"

Little Owl smiled and put a finger under Alice's chin. "No, I don't," she said. "Your wisdom will take you far."

Over her head, the old woman's eyes found Finn's. "Don't let pride keep you from the home your heart has found." He ducked his head and reached out awkwardly to pat the older woman's shoulder.

Rommy blinked back more tears, and before they could fall, she took Alice's hand. "Let's let Tiger Lily say goodbye without an audience."

She, Alice, and Finn stepped out of the tent. The sun had set long ago. Rommy looked up at the lavender moon. The stars were starting to wink on, their soft song humming in the breeze. It was hard to believe that by this time tomorrow she might be on her way back to London. Despite the beauty here, she wouldn't miss it. Well, maybe the singing stars.

Chapter 23:
Death by Plant

Rommy hovered halfway up the cliff face. Tiger Lily, who couldn't fly, was clinging to the rock face, her feet wedged into separate niches in the rock and her hand gripping an outcropping. She pointed to a nearby plant. The quarter moon gave enough light to see the greenish-blue vine that was wrapped around another plant.

Unfortunately, that plant held blood-red flowers that were all too familiar to Rommy. On her first day in Neverland, she had watched one of those blooms ingest a small bird. The image still made her shudder.

"What do you..."

Tiger Lily put her finger to her lips. "Keep your voice low," she said. "We do not want to wake the blood lilies."

Rommy made a face. "What do you want me to do?" she asked, her voice lowered to a whisper.

"You need to unwrap the fish weed, and I'll cut it off," she said. "It would be best if the lilies do not wake."

Rommy nodded. She flew closer, her hand hovering next to a lily's thick stem. Drawing in a breath, she found the top of the fish weed—right next to a lily blossom almost as big as her forearm. Great. Just great.

She gingerly worked her finger under the edge of the fish weed vine and started to uncoil it from the other plant's stem. The blossom shifted, and Rommy froze. She didn't move until it was completely still again.

Carefully, she returned to unwinding the tiny vine. She got all the way to the end, and Tiger Lily leaned over and snipped the vine off, putting it in a bag at her waist. She nodded to the next plant. Rommy repeated the process with three more vines. Besides a few twitches that had Rommy's heart in her throat, the blossoms slumbered on.

As she started on the fourth vine, some of the tension in her shoulders released. It seemed as long as she was careful, the plants wouldn't bother them.

"How much of this do we need?" Rommy asked, her voice soft.

Tiger Lily shifted, getting a better grip. Her mouth pressed into a thin line. "A lot more than we have," she said. "You need to move faster."

Rommy frowned at her. She couldn't help thinking about the remaining leaf in her pocket. Being able to wish the fish weed into Tiger Lily's bag would be a lot quicker, not to mention less stressful. But she couldn't see how she'd be able to do that without explaining the leaves to Tiger Lily. The older girl had proven to be an unexpected ally, but Rommy wasn't ready to entrust the other girl with her biggest secret.

"I'm trying," Rommy said, "but this fish weed isn't the easiest thing to get off of here. With this moon, it's a little hard to see the end of the vines."

Tiger Lily gave a terse nod. "Just go as fast as you can."

Rommy finished unwrapping the last of the vines on the blood lily in front of her. After Tiger Lily had cut it off and put in the bag with the rest, she tucked her blade away and moved sideways toward another plant.

Slowly the two girls made their way around the cliff face. Rommy carefully unwound the fish weed vine, and Tiger Lily would cut it off and put it in her bag. Rommy had lost track of the number of plants they had divested of the tiny vine, but it felt like she had been unwinding plants for half the night. She had no idea how Tiger Lily moved from place to place or what kind of strength it took to keep holding on for this long. A few places had rocky outcroppings large enough for the older to girl to perch, but still.

"One more," said Tiger Lily, nodding at a plant that clung higher than the rest. The cliff face almost seemed to bend outward, and Rommy didn't know how in the world Tiger Lily thought she could climb up there and hold on. Despite Rommy's misgivings, Tiger Lily crawled over the cliff face like a spider, her feet and hands unerringly finding the right holds.

This plant was bigger than the rest. Instead of the three to five large blossoms the other plants had, this one had at least seven. Rommy had shed her nerves after the second plant. She quickly got to work on the first vine. She had almost completely unwound it when the blossom twitched. Her fingers stilled as she waited for it to settle again.

When she resumed her unwinding, the blossom and its neighbor shivered. Rommy glanced at Tiger Lily.

"Keep going," the older girl hissed at her. "We need those vines."

Rommy hesitated and then started gently untwisting the fish weed. Without any warning, the blossom attached to the stem twisted toward her, its petals opening and closing. She jerked back. Several of the other blossoms began to shiver and shake back and forth.

Tiger Lily leaned away from the plant that was now lunging in her direction. "Sing," she said.

Rommy stared at her. "Sing? What am I supposed to sing?"

"Just do it," said Tiger Lily through gritted teeth. She had swung backward out of the blossoms' reach, but she had had to take one foot off the rock to do it. Her body hung at a precarious angle.

Rommy sang the first song that popped into her mind which was her school's song. It was an upbeat, march-like tune. The blossoms began to wag in time to the beat of the song, but they didn't look any less awake. In fact, now all but one of the blossoms were waving back and forth.

Tiger Lily glared at Rommy. "Don't you know anything softer?" she asked.

Rommy's mind went completely blank, and she stopped singing.

The blossoms shook themselves back and forth and then began lunging at both Rommy and Tiger Lily. Rommy could easily avoid them, but Tiger Lily wasn't so lucky. She had put her knife between her teeth and was trying to scramble, crablike, away from the plant.

Rommy started to hum mindlessly in an effort to calm the flower, but it was too late. The message must have traveled through the roots to the other plants because now they were all waking up across the cliff face. Tiger Lily was hemmed in on all sides by lunging flowers, and they still needed more vines.

"Hang on," said Rommy. She pulled her own dagger out and approached the waving blossoms. If she could just get in there and cut it off by the root, Tiger Lily could climb to safety, and they'd have the vines they needed.

Rommy darted forward, and a blossom narrowly missed closing on her arm. She sliced at it and it shrank back, but another blossom attacked from below. It closed over her foot. She felt a sharp pain but slashed downward, aiming her dagger at the root. The blossom attached to her foot loosened and fell to the sand below.

The other blossoms start writhing in a fury, and Rommy reached in again, her dagger separating the plant from its roots.

A scream pierced the air, and Rommy whirled in time to see Tiger Lily's hand slip off the rock she was clinging to. Her arms cartwheeled as she began to fall.

Rommy reached out and grabbed the other girl's hand. Her weight dragged them both toward the beach below. Rommy dropped her own dagger, and using her other hand, grabbed Tiger Lily's wrist, flying upward as hard as she could. Their descent slowed and then stopped.

By this time, Tiger Lily had wrapped her other hand around Rommy's. Slowly and with great effort Rommy lowered them both down to the pink sand below. When they touched down, both of their legs gave out, and they collapsed on the sand.

A soft thwack sounded to her right. When Rommy looked over, the blood lily lay on the sand, its blooms limp.

She turned to look at Tiger Lily. "At least we have the vines we need."

All the other girl could manage was a nod before she covered her face with shaking hands.

Rommy left Tiger Lily to recover while she went to retrieve her dagger and get the rest of the fish weed.

Once she was done, she returned to where Tiger Lily now sat. She put her hand on the older girl's shoulder. "Are you all right?" she asked.

Tiger Lily nodded. "I...Thank you," she said. "I thought I was going to meet my ancestors."

Rommy let out a shaky laugh. The adrenaline had drained away, and she was trembling. "Yes, well, I thought we were both goners there for a moment, but we made it." She held up a half dozen fish weed vines. "And we got what we needed." She handed them over to Tiger Lily who put them in her bag. "How long do these last, anyway?"

Tiger Lily shrugged. "It depends on how fresh they are and how strong the plant was that was hosting it."

Rommy smiled. "Then I want the ones from that last plant," she said.

Her mouth tipped up in a smile, Tiger Lily said, "If the spirits smile on us, we will have about half an hour. If they don't..." She shrugged again.

"Do you think that will be long enough?"

Tiger Lily met her eyes. "It will have to be."

A wave of exhaustion swept over Rommy. "We should probably rest while we can." She looked up at the sky. The stars were still shining brightly. "I don't know how long it is until sunrise, but the others will be here soon."

Tiger Lily didn't say anything, but she started to gather the sand until a small mound was heaped up on the sand. Seeing Rommy staring at her, Tiger Lily pointed. "A few hours rest will help, and the sand is soft."

Rommy followed her example to make her own pink heap of sand. Lying down, she pillowed her head in her arms. Tiger Lily's even breathing told her the other girl had dropped off to sleep. The water made a rhythmic sound as it washed onto shore, and the stars were singing overhead. It was the last thing Rommy heard.

Chapter 24:
Like a Bad Penny

It was still dark when Rommy felt someone shaking her shoulder. She blinked open her eyes. In the dim light, Francie's face came into view. A sense of déjà vu swept over Rommy. For a moment, she was back at Chattingham's before this whole adventure had started. Little had she known when she sneaked out everything that awaited her outside the gates of her boarding school.

Rommy sat up and rubbed her eyes. The last of the stars winked out as she watched, its song fading away. She got to her feet. The others were already up and waiting. Rommy's eyes ran over those gathered. She and Francie were from upper-class London. Finn and Alice were from the lower class. The Lost Boys were most likely from a mix of middle and upper classes, and then there was Tiger Lily with her copper skin, black eyes, and even blacker hair. Add in four fairies, and it was an odd assortment by anyone's assessment.

Tiger Lily was kneeling with the others surrounding her. She was pulling out tendrils of fish weed. She handed a wad to Finn and turned to Rommy, another wad in her hand.

"Wait until right before you go into the water," she said. "As I told you, this only lasts so long. I gave you enough so that you can chew a second wad if you need it."

Rommy stared down at the tangled strings of blue-green vines. She wondered how it worked, and if she'd end up with gills or fins.

Francie put her hands on her hips. "Why can't I help?" she asked. She looked at Rommy. "You know I can swim, and you need me. Finn said there are three mermaids, so three of us besides you should go." She tossed her black curls over her shoulder.

Ever since she had rescued Francie, there had been a hum of tension between them. Besides Francie's overt flirting with Finn, Francie seemed different here. Back at Chattingham's, Francie was always on Rommy's side. Now Rommy wasn't so sure. She looked at her friend's snapping dark eyes and wondered which one of them had changed more.

Holding up a hand, she said, "I know you're a marvelous swimmer, Francie, but this is different. You haven't met the mermaids. They aren't like the stories we've read."

Francie crossed her arms. "I know that! I'm not stupid. You've all been talking about how to get around them, and Finn was telling me how vicious they can be."

Rommy pushed down her irritation. "This isn't a game we're playing. Those mermaids will try to kill you." She shook her head. "No, Francie, you can't go. It's too risky."

Francie stepped closer to Rommy and jutted her chin out. "Who died and put you in charge, anyway? How come you get to say who does what?"

Finn pushed between them and put a restraining hand on Francie's arm. "Rommy is the one that almost died, more'n once, and this is her quest. Unilisi talked to her, not us, and certainly not you," said Finn.

Francie jerked her arm away. The look she gave Rommy was a combination of hurt and anger.

"Fine," she said and plopped down on a rock. "I'd rather stay here, anyway."

"Francie," said Rommy starting toward her, but Alice grabbed her arm.

"Let her stew," she said. "We've got bigger fish to fry." She pointed toward the horizon, which showed a faint glow.

Rommy sighed and looked over at her friend who had turned further away, her back stiff. They'd have to settle things later.

She, Finn, and Tiger Lily walked toward the water. Rommy had taken off her boots. When the water began to lap at her feet, she shoved a wad of the plant into her mouth, tucking the rest into the pocket of her pants. She chewed and had to fight from gagging. The fish weed tasted like fish—very old, smelly fish. She kept chewing and forced herself to swallow.

She saw Finn and Tiger Lily lift their hands when suddenly a loud crowing sound carried to them on the breeze. Rommy's eyes widened as she, Finn, and Tiger Lily spun toward the sound.

Peter Pan was flying toward them, the remaining Lost Boys in his wake. He landed on the beach, and before anyone could think to move, he had grabbed Walter.

"How rude!" he said. "After all, I've done for you, why would you leave?" He jerked Walter tighter and pulled his dirk.

Rommy heard Finn turn and splash back to shore. Tiger Lily also leaped toward the shore and knocked the bow and arrow out of a tall Lost Boy's hands. Rommy thought it was Oscar, but she wasn't sure because something was happening to her. She was breathing in, but her lungs started to scream for air. No matter how frantically she pulled in air, nothing seemed to be happening. She felt something tickle her neck, and her hand flew to the spot.

Small flaps were layered on either side. Gills. The fish weed had worked. Looking at the chaos on the beach, Rommy knew she didn't have a choice. She had to go underwater, or she'd die. Of course, she might die anyway. As she splashed forward and dove into the water, she thought she saw something catch the light off to her right.

Underwater, Rommy drew in a long breath through her nose. Salt water stung and brought tears to her eyes. For a moment, she thought Tiger Lily might have double-crossed them, but then air filled her lungs. She took in several more deep watery breaths, and the spinning in her head stopped.

She wasn't sure where the Cave of Sighs was, but since it was a cave, she knew it couldn't be in the center of the lagoon. It must be somewhere along the coast where the rocky cliffs embraced the lagoon waters.

Rommy found she could see as clearly underwater as on land. It must be the fish weed. As she rushed by a large tangle of purple and blue coral reef, she startled several fish. In her mind, she felt their surprise and a few pops of annoyance. Apparently, fish weed enabled you to do more than breathe underwater.

A golden light was starting to spread across the waves when she reached the far edge of the lagoon. It was dotted with caverns. There were at least four caves that were large enough that she couldn't see to the back of them. As she examined them in turn, she caught movement out of the corner of her eye. Turning, she saw a mermaid with long black hair streaming behind her. Wasn't her name Adela?

"*Very good, Human,*" said a voice in her head. "*I'm surprised you remembered. Humans usually only worry about themselves.*" The mermaid swam around Rommy, reminding her once again of a shark.

"*Did you come to play?*" another voice sounded in Rommy's head. She twisted around to find the golden-haired mermaid Arista on her other side.

Rommy offered a smile. Now that she was here, she wasn't sure what to do.

"*Well, if you don't know what you're doing, we certainly don't.*" The blonde's giggle flowed through the water. She turned to her sister. "*I didn't know humans had such open minds. This could be so much fun.*" She circled closer to Rommy, who backed away, only to find herself bumping into Adela.

Rommy felt an uncomfortable sensation in her mind, like someone was rummaging around. She mentally shoved the feeling away.

"*Hey!*" Arista's blue eyes narrowed. "*You could have just asked us to leave your mind. No need to get pushy.*"

Rommy mentally imagined a wall around her mind. Sudden silence descended. The two mermaids swam in a tighter circle, but Rommy couldn't hear them at all. Maybe her mental walls were too high. She imagined a small window, and the mermaids' thoughts once again became audible again.

"You are trespassing in our lagoon, Human." Adela's green eyes were cold. *"Do you know what we do with trespassers?"*

"Nothing good, probably." Rommy smiled cheerfully.

Adela blinked.

The blonde laughed. *"She might be more fun than I thought. Why did you come to visit us, then?"* She flicked her tail and did a pirouette. *"I don't think it was to come play."*

An idea popped into Rommy's mind, and she pushed the words toward them. *"They told me that there was a Cave of Sighs, but that's just an old wives' tale. How would you ever have collected sighs, anyway?"*

Adela let out a screeching sound that made Rommy's head ring. *"What do you mean mermaids can't collect sighs? We have collected every last sigh in the whole sea."*

Rommy shrugged and tried to look bored. *"I'll believe it when I see it."*

The light from the sunrise was turning the water from deep indigo to tourmaline. She had to hurry. If she could just get into the Cave of Sighs.

Arista let out a peal of laughter. *"You are always too sensitive, Adela. Let's show the human. We can always kill her later."*

Rommy tried not to react to the casual reference to her death. Adela flicked her tail and was in Rommy's face. Rommy fought the urge to back away. She had a feeling Adela would pounce on any weakness like the shark she resembled.

The mermaid sneered. *"Are you sure you want to go into our cave, Human? Nobody will ever find your bones."*

"Are you afraid to show me your cave, Mermaid?" Rommy let her own lip curl.

"Come, Arista, let's show the human our wonders before she dies."

Grasping Rommy's wrist she began swimming, yanking Rommy along behind her. Rommy felt itching along her neck. Using her free hand, she felt her neck. The flaps were shrinking. She dug her hand into her pocket and pulled out another wad of fish weed. She stuffed it into her mouth and chewed with quiet franticness. She swallowed it down without either mermaid noticing. Fortunately, Adela was too busy towing her along, and Arista was playing in the waves.

Adela pulled her into the cave farthest to the right, and Rommy knew as soon as she entered why it was called the Cave of Sighs. Colorful bubbles floated through the water. From each one came the sound of a sigh. Some were high-pitched, and some were low, and they swirled around her until her vision was filled with the colorful orbs. It was disorientating.

Adela let go of her wrist and crossed her arms, watching for Rommy's reaction. Rommy didn't have to act. The effect of all those voices contained in the rainbow of floating bubbles was both a nightmare and a wonder.

In addition to the colorful orbs floating everywhere, lanterns intricately carved with swirling seashells hung in niches on the sides of the cave. Along one wall were what looked like large conch shells. One of the shells opened to reveal a brilliantly pink cushion. The redheaded mermaid swam out of it.

"Sisters?" Her quiet question echoed in the cave. When she saw Rommy her golden eyes widened. She looked at her sisters. *"Why is a human here?"*

While Adela answered the youngest sister's questions, Rommy looked around for the door. Toward the back of the cave were two stone pillars that looked familiar. She eased her way toward them.

Arista swam next to her. *"Would you like the tour?"* She giggled, but her blue eyes were cold. *"You wouldn't want to die without seeing it all, would you?"*

Rommy nodded, hoping the mermaid would bring her closer to the door. Arista swam through the throng of colored bubbles. She gently swatted first one and then another, telling which shipwreck each came from and whose last sigh was contained within.

Rommy followed her and had to suppress a shiver. In her head, she could hear a clock ticking and knew if she didn't do something soon, her last sigh would be floating in this cave, too.

She could see the door. A plain keyhole was in the center of an iron panel. It was outlined in darker iron fretwork. Rommy pointed at an indigo-colored orb that was floating right in front of the door. *"Whose sigh is that? It's such a dark blue."*

Arista's eyes lit up. *"Oh yes."* Her smile make a shudder run up Rommy's back. *"That is the last sigh of dear John. He would come visit me, and one day, he stayed."*

While Arista was talking, Rommy had slid over until her back was against the door. She held the key in her hand behind her back, and she was slowly floating upward. The key skidded across the decorative iron that outlined the lock, but she couldn't find the opening.

Arista whirled around toward her. Her eyes narrowed. *"What are you doing? Come away from there."*

"John?" Rommy hoped to distract the mermaid while she fished around trying to find the keyhole. *"Who was John? Was he a Lost Boy?"*

"Hmmm? No, he wasn't a Lost Boy. He and his sister and younger brother came to Neverland." Her mouth curved into a smile. *"Only the sister and younger brother left. Dear John stayed with me."* She batted the indigo bubble playfully and a long sigh emerged from it.

Suddenly, the mermaid's eyes sharpened, and she swam closer. *"Come away from there, Human."*

"What do you mean, he stayed with you?" Rommy scrabbled desperately behind her back to find the keyhole.

"He died." The mermaid let out an exasperated sigh. She was now right in front of Rommy. She reached out a claw-like hand and gripped Rommy's upper arm, jerking her away from the door.

The key slipped from Rommy's grasp and swirled toward the floor of the cave. Rommy stared into Arista's eyes, not daring to even peek at the key in the hopes the mermaid hadn't seen it.

Arista's blue eyes glittered like glass. *"I think you've seen enough. It's time to play a little game called 'I wonder what color your sigh will be.'"* A predatory smile curved her lips.

"I've always liked green. You know, that deep bottle green?"

Arista blinked in surprise, and Rommy took the opportunity to yank away from the mermaid. She dove to the floor, kicking out with one leg to push the mermaid away. Her fingers closed around the key, and she whirled back toward the door. She felt a burning pain as the mermaid's long fingernails raked down her back, but Rommy jammed the key into the hole. She turned it in the lock once and then twice before Arista was on her.

The mermaid tried to slide her arm around Rommy's throat, but Rommy ducked her chin, blocking the move. Arista still managed to yank her backwards, and the key slipped out of Rommy's reach. She bucked and twisted, and her fingers grazed the edge of the key before Arista pulled her further back.

The mermaid was too strong, and Rommy knew she'd never be able to out muscle her. She stopped straining toward the key, surprising Arista into pausing. Rommy took advantage of the mermaid's hesitation and scrabbled in her pocket for the wish leaf, pulling it out. She could only pray this would work.

Grasping the leaf in her hand, she spoke out loud, her words forming bubbles in the water. "I wish for the key in the lock to turn once more."

For a moment, Rommy thought it hadn't worked, but with a low creak, the key twisted the third and final time.

The door began to glow, and Arista stopped her attack to stare. The glow turned into a pulsing power that swelled outward until it shoved both Rommy and Arista tumbling away from the door.

"What have you done?" The blonde's screech was like nails in Rommy's head. Arista's pupils narrowed to slits, and the golden hair around her head writhed in a frenzy.

Rommy dodged the mermaid's outstretched fingers and swam for all she was worth toward the mouth of the cave.

She was only feet away from the opening when Adrina loomed up in front of her. Rommy tried to dodge past her, but the redhead pushed a small pipe-like instrument into her hand.

"Play this. The dolphins will hear and take you to the shore."

"But...why?" Rommy couldn't help the question.

Two perfect tears welled up in the mermaid's whiskey-gold eyes. *"John didn't visit Arista. He visited me."* The two tears fell in perfect glittering trails down her cheeks. The mermaid caught one on her fingertip and touched Rommy's back. The pain that had been pulsing just under Rommy's awareness faded. Then Adrina pushed Rommy toward the cave entrance. *"Go. I will distract them."*

"Thank you." Rommy grasped the small flute and swam as fast as she could. She cleared the entrance and swam out into the lagoon's impossibly blue waters. She'd only gotten several yards when her neck started to itch.

Chapter 25:
Friends Reunited

No, no, no. Rommy headed toward the surface. When her head broke the water, the beach seemed very far away. Dawn streaked fingers of light across the ocean. She had done it. She had turned the key.

Her sense of elation quickly ebbed, though. She was stuck on the far side of the lagoon, and she was out of fish weed. She squinted at the beach. From here, she couldn't see what was happening. She kicked her feet and started to swim toward the beach. She needed to get farther away from the cave and its murderous mermaids.

She had only swum a few feet when something jerked on her foot. She kicked with all her might and felt a satisfying thud of her foot connecting with flesh. She made it another few feet when she was yanked completely underwater.

Arista's teeth were bared in a grin. Rommy tried to bring the flute to her mouth, but Arista gripped her wrist. The mermaid was impossibly strong, and in the water she had the advantage.

Rommy's lungs begged for air. She kicked out with her feet and managed to connect with the mermaid's scale-covered stomach. Unfortunately, it only seemed to make her angrier.

Arista started to drag Rommy toward the bottom of the lagoon. Black spots danced in front of Rommy's eyes. She knew she didn't have long until she would pass out. And then she'd be dead. In a last desperate bid, she stopped trying to pull away from Arista and allowed the mermaid to pull her close. As their faces came closer, she noticed the mermaid's blue eyes had strangely elongated pupils. Rommy stared into those cold blue eyes and with her last bit of strength, she reared back and smacked her forehead into the mermaid's nose.

Arista let go of Rommy and grabbed her face. Rommy kicked her legs and shot toward the surface. She got one blessed lungful of air before she was pulled under again. The mermaid wrapped her arms round Rommy, pinning her arms to her sides. Rommy kicked as hard as she could, but it was impossible. She clenched the flute in her hand. If only she could bring it to her mouth.

Her lungs were burning again. Tears sprang to her eyes. She was going to die in this lagoon, and she'd never see Papa again. Worse, would everyone be stuck here in Neverland forever? Her vision was going dark, and she twisted hard to the left. Suddenly, she was released, and someone was pulling her up. Then, her face broke through the surface.

Air! Air flowed into her lungs. Someone was shoving something into her mouth. Rommy almost spit it out but a hand covered her mouth and nose. She thrashed back and forth. Was the other mermaid trying to kill her now, after playing with her?

She chewed and swallowed the nasty thing in her mouth. Fish weed. She drew in a long breath and Francie's face came into view. She felt the familiar itching and let Francie pull her back under the water, drawing in a salty breathe.

"Come on," Francie's voice resounded in her head. *"We have to get away from that creature. I think I only wounded her."*

It was then that Rommy realized tendrils of red were spreading through the water. *"And that blood might bring something worse, too."* She looked past Francie's shoulder into the endless blue behind her where the open ocean lay.

Francie grasped her hand and began swimming toward the beach. Rommy pulled on her. Francie came to a stop, and Rommy held up the flute. Francie's face scrunched in confusion.

"It's our ride back." Rommy put the flute to her mouth and blew a few notes. She didn't hear anything. They both waited for several seconds. Rommy blew again, but Francie grabbed her hand again.

"We can't wait around, Rommy. We have to get away from those nasty mermaids, and this fish weed won't last forever."

Rommy felt a sinking disappointment. The redheaded mermaid had seemed sincere. Maybe whoever the flute was supposed to call was busy or too far away. Whatever the reason, Francie was right. They needed to head back.

The two of them kicked off toward the shore. Suddenly, sleek dark turquoise bodies appeared on either side of them. A cheerful series of chirps and clicks sounded through the water.

"Hello, I'm Delphia." The voice came from the creature on Rommy's right. *"We heard your song, and we're here to answer it. What can we do for you?"*

Rommy heard Francie's gasp and the two girls' eyes met. Francie was the first to recover, a grin spreading over her face. Even underwater, her dark eyes sparkled.

"We sure would." Francie turned to the creature next to her, a sleek dolphin, its body a brilliant turquoise that faded to the palest blue on its underside.

The creature dipped lower. *"I'm Willis. Here, grab on, and your friend can do the same to Delphia. Where do you want to go?"*

Rommy and Francie each reached for a fin. Rommy's grasp was hesitant. The dolphin let out a series of clicks. *"You'll never be able to hold on that way."* Delphia. bobbed back and forth. *"It's okay. You won't hurt me or anything. Just grab on nice and tight."*

The other dolphin let out a high-pitched chirp and a moment later a similar sound echoed back at them. *"You'd best hurry it up. Dover says the mermaid is recovering."*

Rommy tightened her grip, and she caught a glimpse of Francie hanging onto Willis before she was zipping through the water. She closed her eyes and hung on for dear life.

Water whipped past her face, and she could feel bubbles tickling her face. Her legs streamed out behind her. She heard Francie let out a whoop, but she concentrated on keeping a tight grip on the cool, slick fin.

The trip across the lagoon seemed to take only seconds, and soon, both dolphins were gliding to a graceful stop. They were still out far enough that Rommy couldn't touch the bottom, but the beach was within easy swimming distance now.

"This is where we stop." Willis gently bumped Francie's shoulder with his nose. Francie's giggle rippled through the water.

Delphia gave a loud click. *"Hope you enjoyed the ride."*

"Thank you." Rommy gently patted the creature's head, hoping it wasn't offensive to do so. The dolphin nodded its head and then chirped to its companion. *"It was a pleasure helping you both."* She turned her head toward the other dolphin. *"Let's go, Willis."*

And with a last click, they were gone.

Rommy and Francie looked at each other, but before either could speak, Francie started scratching at her neck. Rommy felt the telltale tickle a moment later. Together, they swam forward. It didn't take long until their feet could touch the ground. They both stood up, and the water came almost to Rommy's chest.

The two girls looked at each other. Rommy threw her arms around Francie.

"Thank you," she said simply. "You saved my life."

Francie pushed her away and smiled. "I told you I would be helpful."

Rommy squeezed her friend's hand. "Yes, I was wrong," said Rommy. "I said you wouldn't be able to help and...and I was wrong."

"Yeah, you were," said Francie with a wink. Then she wrinkled her nose. "But I'm sorry too. I...I've not really been on your side, have I?" She impulsively pulled Rommy back into a hug.

Rommy squeezed her back. "It's okay. Things have been kind of overwhelming for all of us, and I..." Rommy pulled away and looked down. She wasn't sure how to explain how she felt about Finn, since she didn't know herself. And then there was Lobo. Could she tell Francie what she'd done? The urge to tell someone, to not have to carry this heavy secret around was almost irresistible.

Then Francie plowed into the pause. "It's just...you've changed, and I wasn't sure how to...that is, it didn't seem like you needed me anymore."

Rommy's eyes widened. "I'll always need you, Francie," she said. "You're my best friend. Besides, I think you just proved you're needed in an epic way."

Francie grinned. "I did, didn't I?" She gave another glance over her shoulder. "Now let's get out of this water before one of those creatures comes after us." She shook her head. "And to think, I used to feel sorry for Hans Andersen's *Little Mermaid*."

Rommy giggled, but she couldn't agree more. Linking her arm in Francie's and pushing her wet hair out of her face, they waded toward the shore together.

Rommy stopped when she was still shin-deep in the water. Alice, Finn, and Tiger Lily were clustered warily on the beach with some of her father's crew. Rommy's eyes widened when she saw their leader lying prone on the beach, Gentleman Jack kneeling at his side.

"Papa!" she cried.

Chapter 26:
Truth If You Dare

Rommy let go of Francie's arm and splashed toward the shore. The group parted as she stumbled through the sand and sank to her father's side.

Gentleman Jack, one of her father's crew, had ripped off his own shirt and had wadded it up. He was pushing it hard into her father's stomach. It took only one glance to see that almost the entire cloth was a deep red.

Rommy's eyes climbed from the shirt to her father's face which was gray in the early morning light. His eyes were closed; his breathing was labored.

Tentatively, she touched her fingers to his face. "Papa?"

Hook's eyes cracked open, and it took him a moment to focus on her face. "Rommy," he said, his voice barely a whisper. "You're...safe." He raised a trembling hand to her face and cupped her cheek. "My...darling...girl."

Rommy closed her hand over his, tears brimming in her eyes. "I'm here, Papa. I'm right here, and you're going to be okay."

A smile ghosted across her father's face. "I...I...don't think so. Not...this time."

His hand fell back to the sand, and he coughed violently. Horror seized Rommy when she saw a small trickle of blood leak from the corner of his mouth.

Once the coughing subsided, her father pried his eyes open again, and she could see the sheen of tears in them. "I...love...you," he rasped out, "don't...ever...believe...I didn't." Each word came with great effort.

Determination washed over Rommy, and she pressed her lips into a tight line. She could feel everyone's eyes on her, but she didn't care. Nobody was dying on her watch again, even if they all ended up hating her. She dug her hand into her pocket and pulled out the last remaining wish leaf. It was wet and drooping.

Shoving Gentleman Jack's hands away, she pushed the cloth off her father's stomach. Blood gurgled out from a long slash.

"No, you can't do that," said Gentleman Jack, trying to shove the cloth back into place. "He's already lost too much blood."

"I can fix it," she said and elbowed the dashing pirate out of the way. She placed the leaf on the wound and held it there with her hand, her father's warm blood staining her fingers. She swallowed hard. Her mind whirred. She had to do this just right because if she didn't...

Closing her eyes, she spoke. "I wish the gash in my father's stomach...I wish it would...stop bleeding and...mend itself...immediately."

The leaf became warm to the touch, and she took her hand off. Just like with Pan, light spilled out from the edges of the leaf. This time cracks spread up the stem and along the veins, and the surface of the leaf turned a dark red, almost black.

Then her father's body began to jerk. He let out a low moan of pain.

Gentleman Jack made a move as if to snatch the leaf off, but Rommy grabbed his arm.

"No, wait," she said.

A moment later, the blood stopped gushing and slowed to a trickle and then stopped all together.

A bright pulse of light glowed out and the leaf dissolved into tiny particles. Like the last time, they drifted upward until they disappeared.

Her father's entire torso was smeared with blood, and she took the handkerchief that Gentleman Jack handed her and wiped it off as best she could. Instead of an open wound, a pink line marked her father's stomach. It looked like an old scar.

A heavy silence fell over the entire group. Rommy could feel everyone's stares.

She ignored them and watched her father's face. His eyes were closed and he was still. Too still. Had she been too late?

Then Hook suddenly took in a great, gasping breath and sat bolt upright, almost knocking Rommy over. His hands went to his middle, and he groped around for a moment, his shirt flapping open.

"What...I don't understand..." He looked from Rommy, down at his torso, and then back at her again.

The tears that had been brimming spilled over her lashes and down her cheeks.

And then she was in his arms, and he was hugging her so tightly she could hardly breathe. For just a moment, everything was right in the world.

Rommy could hear everyone talking and the questions flying, but she clung to her father. Her tears flowing fast and thick, soaking his shoulder.

"Oh, my dear," he said, as he finally set at arms' length. He cupped her cheek in his hand. "I thought I would never see you again. I thought I'd die on this cursed island, and you'd be left here..." his voice broke, and he ran the back of his sleeve across his eyes.

She covered his hand. "But that didn't happen, Papa," she said, sniffling. "You're all right now, and we're going to leave here, together."

He reached out and crushed her back to his chest. "I was wrong, Rommy," he said. He spoke into her hair. "I was wrong to stay here all this time, trying to avenge your brother's death. You needed me, and I wasn't there for you. If I had died..." he paused and cleared his throat several times, "you could have been marooned here forever."

Her face was pressed against his shoulder, making it hard to speak. She gently pushed herself away and sat back on knees. "But you didn't die, and we're not going to be stuck here forever." A smile broke across her face, and she swiped at her eyes. "The only person who will be stuck here forever is Pan."

Her father frowned at her. "Whatever do you mean, my dear?" He looked around the circle surrounding them. "And however did you manage to collect so many children in such a short amount of time?"

So, she told him. She told him about their trip to the jungle, and Unilisi's instructions. She told him that she had turned the key in the lock, and they all had until the next sunrise to leave or risk getting sealed here with Pan forever. The whole time she talked, Rommy kept her eyes resolutely on her father's face. She could feel the others pressing forward, could almost hear the questions Alice was bursting to ask, but she ignored them. For now.

When she got done, her father ran a hand over his face. "I should be angry with you," he said and then shook his head. "But this entire situation is my fault. If it wasn't for my stubbornness, for my insistence on revenge, you'd never have come to Neverland to begin with." Then, he slapped his hands on his thighs and with one smooth movement, he rolled onto his feet. He extended his hook toward Rommy. When she grasped it, he hauled her to her feet.

Her father looked around at the expectant faces that surrounded them. "It looks like we have our work cut out for us," he said. When nobody moved, he snorted. "Well, what are you all staring at? Big Red, Max, gather something to start a fire with, and Smee, quit gawping and take Gentleman Jack to catch us something to eat." Hook gestured at Finn and at the Lost Boys. "You lot keep out of the way." A grin spread over his face, and he patted his stomach with his good hand. "Nothing like almost getting gutted to stir a man's appetite."

Her father's men scattered to do her father's bidding, and Hook put his arm around Rommy again and hugged her to him.

She tipped her face up. "I need to make sure these scalawags follow directions," he said. He touched her chin with the edge of his hook. "Why don't you get yourself cleaned up a bit. There'll be time for plans once we get some food for this lot."

She smiled at him. Already she could feel the adrenaline draining away. Her legs felt watery, but she locked her knees. She needed to tell her friends about the horrible things she'd done without her father watching.

"You're right, Papa," she said and dredged up a smile. "I'll do that." With a last squeeze, he let her go and strode off after his men.

Rommy turned on trembling legs and almost ran into Alice.

"Ya look like someone gutted *you*," the little girl said, wrinkling her nose.

Rommy looked down to see her father's blood was smeared on the sleeves of her shirt. Added to the stains on her hands, she looked like she was the one with a deadly wound. Rommy stomach pitched at the sight of all that blood, and she swallowed hard.

She pushed past Alice and stumbled toward the water's edge. "I'm sorry," she said. "I need to get this...this off me."

She fell to her knees in the surf and stuck her arms into the cool water up to her elbows. The waves washed away the red, until her hands were clean and her shirt sleeves had faded to a dull pink.

Once again tears brimmed up in her eyes. She didn't know if she could face it, face them. They'd all hate her now. She knew that, but it had been worth it to save her father. She sniffed and lifted a dripping hand to wipe at her face.

She felt a small hand pat her back and a bigger hand clasp her shoulder. "Are ya okay?" Alice squatted down next to her and peered into her face.

Rommy squeezed her eyes shut and drew in a long, shuddering breath. Then she pushed back to her feet. She turned toward the other girls and Finn. The Lost Boys were huddled behind him. They all looked worried.

Francie moved to put an arm around her shoulder, but Rommy stepped back. She could hardly bear to look at them, but she made herself look into each face. "I suppose you're wondering what happened, how I did that," she said.

"I've never seen anything like that," Francie interrupted, her eyes alive with excitement. "What kind of leaf was that anyway? You should take some of those home with us!"

"I can't," said Rommy. "That...that was the last one." Her lips trembled and she pushed them together. "Unilisi gave me three leaves, wish leaves."

"Wish leaves?" asked Finn after a beat of silence. "Why didn't you say anything before now?"

Rommy opened her mouth, but Alice jumped in. "You had them wish leaves when we was leaving the jungle?" The younger girl's face scrunched up in confusion.

Rommy nodded, and then she answered the unspoken question that hung in the air. "I could have saved Lobo," she said, her voice catching. "I could have saved him, but...but I forgot I had them."

A stunned silence fell over the group.

Rommy didn't want to see the disappointment, the disgust, and she dropped her eyes to the sand. Tears began flowing down her face.

"I...I'm so sorry," she said. "I...I came out of the grove, and...and I had to run...before the guardian trees closed...the opening." A sob rose up and choked her. "By the time...Pan...killed Lobo..." She was crying now so hard she could hardly speak. "I forgot...I had them...until Little Owl...she gave us the stones."

Rommy wrapped her arms around her middle, trying to keep herself from flying apart. "It's all my fault...he's dead," she said. Her voice dropped to a whisper. "I could have saved him, but...I didn't."

She covered her face with her hands as great sobs shook her body. Finn was the first to move. He stepped toward her and put his arms around her.

"It's not your fault," he said. "It's Pan's fault. He's the one that shot Lobo. Not you."

"But..but...I had the leaves...and," Rommy gulped in air.

Finn pressed his cheek into her hair and he rubbed a hand along her back. "Everyone makes mistakes," he said, "even you. We know you loved Lobo as much as me and Alice."

Alice tugged at her arm, and Rommy pulled away from Finn to look at her. "How many of them leaves did ya have?" Alice asked.

Rommy had to clear her throat twice before she could speak. "Three, I had three of them."

"And you used the last one on the Captain?" asked Finn.

Rommy nodded her head. "I used one to take the poison out of Pan's wound, and I had to use one to get the key turned the final time. This was the last one I had."

Alice slipped her arms around Rommy's waist. "I loved Lobo," she said, "and I know you loved him too. But iffen you had used one of them leaves on Lobo, maybe you wouldn't have had any left to save yer old man." Alice sniffed. "I know Lobo wouldn't have wanted that."

Francie grabbed Rommy's hand. "I don't know who Lobo was, but I know it would have killed you to watch your father die on this beach," she said. "Maybe you were supposed to forget so you'd have one left to save him."

Rommy wiped at her red, swollen eyes. She squeezed Francie's hand. "Thank you," she said. "I never thought of it like that."

Finn put his an arm around her shoulders and she leaned her head against him. The cold ball of dread that had taken up permanent residence in her heart slowly began to dissolve. Her friends didn't hate her after all. They had not only forgiven her, but they made her see things in a different way. She would always be sad that Lobo died, but Francie was right, too. What if she hadn't had any way to save her father? She shuddered at the thought.

Rommy blinked tears out of her eyes and met Finn's gaze. He winked at her. "Next time, though, maybe you should have a little more faith in your friends," he said. "You don't have to carry everything all by yourself all the time."

Rommy thought back to what Little Owl had said, how part of her strength came from her friends. Her smile was a bit wobbly.

"I won't," she promised.

Chapter 27:

Going Home Just Got Complicated

Big Red built a roaring fire on the beach while several of the other men caught enough fish for the entire group. Smee, who had beached the small boat the crew had used to reach Mermaid Lagoon, carefully cooked the fish over the fire, while Max went off to forage for some fruit.

After the big reveal on the beach, Francie decided Max needed help finding enough fruit for everyone. He didn't seem to mind, from the way he was grinning at her, his blond-streaked head bent toward her. Soon the entire group, both pirates and children, were gathered around the fire, eating a breakfast of roasted fish and cloud berries which grew along the cliffs. Rommy sat next to her father, her shoulder touching his. It still shook her to realize how close she'd come to losing him. Glancing around, she realized the fairies were nowhere to be found.

After taking the last bite of her fish, Rommy wiped her mouth with the back of her hand. She wrinkled her nose. She hoped she'd have the opportunity to get cleaned up soon. The ocean had washed off the slimy mud from the salt marshes, but now her clothes were stiff from the salt water. She eyed the others. Of course, nobody else looked much better.

"Now," said her father, slapping his knees, "tell me again how much time is left until the Neverland passage is closed?"

"Until the next sunrise, Papa," said Rommy.

Big Red grunted. "And ya say that iffen we don't go with ye now, we'll be stuck here, forever?"

Rommy nodded.

"If you closed the passage, isn't there a way to reopen it?" asked Gentleman Jack.

"That tree person said you can't," said Alice and shrugged.

Rommy added, "I'm not exactly sure why, but from what Unilisi said, it seems the passage can only ever be opened once and closed once."

Her father raised an eyebrow. "Unilisi is this, this...tree person?"

A smile tugged at Rommy's mouth. "I don't know that you'd call her a person exactly, but she is the island's source of magic." She shrugged. "I'm not sure how it all works. All I know is that we had to get the key and go to the Cave of Sighs and turn it in the lock. Now that that's done, we have until the next sunrise to leave. Whoever is left on the island won't be able to leave—ever."

"I suppose we can't leave immediately because of Pan?" Hook asked.

"The idea is to seal him here, while we leave," said Rommy. "He knows what we're about, so he could try to get off the island, too."

Tiger Lily spoke up for the first time. "Peter will not want to leave Neverland," she said, "not permanently. His magic will fade in your world, and he will get older, eventually dying. Peter has a great fear of death, and he's been so long with magic, I don't think he could survive without it."

Rommy met her father's eyes over the flickering flames and an understanding flowed between them. "I believe he'll try to stop us, to somehow keep us here," said Hook. "We'll need to stay long enough to ensure he doesn't leave the island, but we shouldn't cut it too close. It'll be a delicate balance. We'll need to make sure the crew is ready to go at a moment's notice."

"But...But...Captain," said Smee. "You can't mean we're going to leave the island?" The small, round man tugged at the wisps of hair on the sides of his almost bald head. "This is our home now."

"Leaving is exactly what I mean to do, Smee," said Hook. "And this cursed place is most certainly not *my* home. If you like it so well, feel free to stay here." Hook's lip curled as he spoke.

"But Capt'n," said Big Red. "Beggin' yer pardon, but I think some of the crew might agree here with old Smee. I don't know that they'll all cotton to leavin' the island, not forever anyways."

Hook's eyebrows lowered, and he glowered at his crewman. "Just what are you saying, Big Red? I would hope I do not have to question your loyalty, too?"

The big man swallowed and shook his head, looking away. Gentleman Jack jumped into the awkward silence. "Captain, of course, we are with you, but be fair. Some of the men have prices on their heads back home or nothing to go back to."

Her father waved his hook. "Then let them stay here with Smee," he said. "I won't force them to leave." He took another bite of his fish.

Gentleman Jack cleared his throat. "Well, Captain, there is the small issue of the ship," he said.

Hook narrowed his eyes. "It is my ship, so I'm not sure wherein the problem lies."

Gentleman Jack tugged at the collar of his shirt with one finger. "Of course, it's your ship, Captain." He gestured toward the other two pirates. "None of us would question that, would we, boys?"

Max and Big Red shook their heads in unison.

"But some of the other men, well, they might, that is to say..."

"Quit tripping over your tongue, Jack," snapped Hook. "Out with it."

Gentleman Jack swallowed hard and then lifted his chin slightly. "Captain, I'm afraid there are some men who would want to stay that might mutiny if you tell them we are leaving with the ship and never coming back."

Hook leaped to his feet, a snarl on his face. The Lost Boys shrank back behind Finn, and Rommy heard someone whimper. Hook ignored the younger boys, his glare full force on Gentleman Jack who was holding up both his hands.

"Now, Captain, you know we're loyal to you, and so's most of the men, but there are a few who are, shall we say, opportunistic."

"Opportunistic?" bellowed Hook. His hand went to one of the swords at his hip. "I'll show them what opportunity has in store for them, if they go against me."

Gentleman Jack pushed to his feet. Rommy couldn't blame him. Her father was a big man and was that much more intimidating when he was looming over you.

"Captain, what I'm saying is, perhaps it would be best to not tell the crew the entire plan." Gentleman Jack raised both eyebrows.

Hook's shoulders relaxed a fraction of an inch. His hand dropped away from his sword, and he rubbed his chin. "You might be right," he said. He narrowed his eyes. "You say there are a few I can't trust. I know Corelli would sooner skewer me than look at me, if given half the chance, but who else do you think would go along with him?" Hook's gaze swung to take in Big Red and then the younger pirate. "And what about you, Max? Or have you been too busy flirting to follow the conversation?"

Max's face turned red, and he straightened away from Francie who had been whispering something in his ear. Francie's face flushed, too, and Rommy saw her scoot away from the young man.

But his grin returned after a moment. "Well, Captain, Sea Hawk has a bounty on his head, so I don't think he'd want to go back," he said. "And Jeb, well, he ain't the sharpest knife in the drawer, if you know what I mean." Max tapped the side of his head and winked.

Hook's lip curled. "That's only three, but it won't do to underestimate Corelli," he said. Hook sank back onto the beach, looking thoughtful. He turned to Rommy and nodded toward her friends. "I suppose all of them will be accompanying us?"

"Yes, Papa, they will," said Rommy.

"Hmmm, that does present a bit of a problem on a number of fronts," said her father as he inspected all of them one by one. Rommy felt a frizzle of nerves when she caught sight of Tiger Lily. Her lips were pressed into a thin line and her eyes were hard. Tiger Lily and the Captain did not have a good history together. She hoped the girl would go along with whatever plan her father came up with.

Her father interrupted her thoughts. "We can't let the crew know this is our last trip from Neverland," he said. "And they'll never believe I just up and decided to take a group of children to London out of the kindness of my heart." He started to pace up and down the beach. An awkward silence fell over the group as they watched him. Finally, he stopped and snapped his fingers.

"Aha! I have it! I will tell them we are going back to London to deliver the lot of you to the workhouse." He pointed his hook in the direction of Finn and the four Lost Boys. He spun and pointed at Tiger Lily. "I'll tell them I am taking you as a favor to your father, to educate you. It is plausible that I would want to reward Chief Hawk Eye for his kindness to my daughter. After all, Captain Hook always repays his debts."

"But, sir, I want to go home," said Walter, shooting to his feet. Tears welled up in his eyes, and his lower lip trembled. "I don't want to go to no poorhouse."

Hook blew out a breath and drew a hand down his face. "Did I *say* you were actually going to the workhouse, Boy? Use your head. I can't say I'm delivering Lost Boys to their homes like so many parcels without raising everyone's suspicions." He closed his eyes for a moment, and when he opened them, one side of his mouth curved up, and he winked at the boy. "Captain Hook doesn't do good deeds like that. I have a reputation to uphold."

Walter stared at him, his mouth slightly ajar. Finn reached up and pulled him back down.

"But Capt'n," said Big Red, "What about the men who would want to stay here if they knew?"

Hook waved a hand in the air. "I'll tell them our trip will be extended and give them the opportunity to stay here," he said. "We can't tell the rest of the crew the truth, or this whole thing could backfire in our faces." He pointed his hook at the group. "That means none of you can share a word of the truth. You will have to play along that you are my prisoners or we may all find ourselves stuck in Neverland forever—or worse."

One by one, everyone around the circle nodded. Rommy hoped this plan of her father's would work. So much depended on the crew believing their story. Would the Lost Boys be able to carry off the ruse until they were truly away from here?

Hook's blue eyes pierced each person's. "If anyone of you lets out the truth, I'll see to it that you are marooned here. Do I make myself clear?"

"But, Papa..."

Hook cut her off with a slice of his hand. "This is important," he said. "If anyone slips up, it will jeopardize us all."

Walter, Jem, Henry, and George all looked at the Captain wide-eyed. Rommy felt Alice grasp her hand, and she squeezed it back. She understood why her father had to be so harsh, but she hoped he would leave Captain Hook behind once they left Neverland.

Smee cleared his throat again, and everyone's eyes swung to him. "But Capt'n, what about the..." he tipped his head out toward the lagoon and then dropped his voice to a stage whisper, "you know."

Chapter 28:

Papa Shows Them the Money

H ook seared Smee with a look, and the older man cringed away from him. "No, Smee, I do not know what you are dithering on about, and neither does anyone else."

Rommy saw Big Red and Gentleman Jack exchange glances, but neither man spoke up.

She looked at her father. He had a thoughtful expression on his face and was staring out at the water. After a moment, he seemed to gather himself. He gestured with his hook toward the boat that Smee had pulled up onto the beach.

"It's quite a row back to the ship," he said. "And the boat will be quite full this time around. We had better get a move on."

Everyone scrambled to their feet while Big Red smothered the fire with some of the pink sand.

"It looks like it'll be a tight fit, Capt'n," he said.

Hook shrugged. "We'll have to just squeeze in," he said. "We don't have time to make more than one trip around to the Cove."

Rommy tugged at her father coat to get his attention. "Won't Finn and the Lost Boys have to look like your captives?

Won't that be difficult if we are all squeezed into the boat together?"

"You do have a point, my dear." He looked down at his ripped and bloodied shirt. "And I will have to explain this." He narrowed his eyes as he surveyed the children of varying sizes clambering into the boat. After a moment, a smile curved over his face. "I think I have an idea, but we'll need to make a stop first."

It didn't take long for everyone to find a seat, although Alice had to sit on Rommy's lap. Walter sat on Finn's lap, and Henry was perched on Tiger Lily's lap, talking a mile a minute. The older girl seemed surprisingly at ease with the little boy.

Rommy's father sat at the bow while the four pirates manned the oars. Their long strokes moved the boat toward the entrance of the lagoon at a steady clip.

Rommy looked out over the lagoon. The sun sparkled on the waves, and gulls called as they swooped and wheeled in the sky. Still, Rommy watched the water uneasily, her eyes peeled for the glitter of mermaid scales.

Francie was squeezed in next to her. She leaned in. "I sure hope those nasty mermaids aren't lurking around here," she said, seeming to read Rommy's mind. "The last thing I want to do is tangle with them again."

Rommy nodded but kept scanning the water. She felt some of the tension leave her body once they were past the entrance to the lagoon. There was no reason that she knew of that the mermaids couldn't leave the lagoon, but still, it felt like they had left their territory, so to speak.

The four men kept up a steady rhythm as the boat bounced across the open water. Outside of the sheltered lagoon, the water was choppier. Rommy felt Alice taking deep breaths.

"Are you okay?" she asked, noticing for the first time that the little girl looked white.

Alice nodded her head, but she continued taking deep breaths and staring out at the horizon. Poor Alice. For someone who didn't like the water, she had been forced into it a lot in recent days.

The Lost Boys and Finn seemed to keep up a constant stream of chatter and Francie joined in, teasing the boys. Tiger Lily engaged little Walter and several times she had the little boy in fits of giggles. Rommy didn't ever remember the older girl smiling so much.

Everyone, even her father, seemed in a buoyant mood, but Rommy couldn't shake the unease that had settled around her shoulders like a damp shawl. She was so deep in her thoughts that she was startled when the boat's bottom bumped on something. Looking up, she realized the men had rowed close to the shore of a small, rocky island. The rocks bore a menacing resemblance to a skull.

Before she could ask where they were or what they were doing. Big Red, Max, Gentleman Jack, and Smee had hopped out of the boat and were guiding the boat through the shallows.

Her father threw over the small anchor and leaped from his spot. The boat bobbed gently in what looked like less than two feet of water. The shore was too rocky to drag the boat onto.

Her father looked at everyone in the boat. "Stay here," he said. "I will be back, and then we'll prepare you to meet my crew." He snapped his fingers. "You men stay with the boat. Smee? Come with me."

Without waiting to see if Smee was following, he strode up onto the rocks and into what looked like the mouth of the skull.

Francie waited until Smee had disappeared behind her father before she jabbed Rommy in her ribs. "What's going on?" she hissed in Rommy's ear.

"I don't know any more than you do," said Rommy.

Tiger Lily was looking after Papa with a frown on her face, and Finn was shaking his head. "It must be true," he said under his breath.

"What do you mean?" asked Rommy.

"I mean, there's been rumors about a treasure that old Captain Hook has squirreled away somewhere." Finn jerked a thumb in the direction of the creepy cave. "I think that's where it is."

Alice wrinkled her nose. "You mean, like buried treasure?"

Finn nodded. "Yep, except it ain't buried exactly."

The Lost Boys murmured to each other.

Rommy glanced uneasily at the three pirates, wondering if they knew about a treasure, and if it could be true. She remembered the look between Gentleman Jack and Big Red when Smee had asked about the "you know what."

How would this complicate things with the other pirates? Or did the other pirates know about the treasure? She had never really thought about why all these men had tied themselves to her father and his ship. The idea that they would care about Papa's revenge for the death of his son at Pan's hands seemed unlikely. She felt like an idiot for not realizing that those men were likely in this life for the treasure.

Before she could voice her concerns to Francie or Alice, her father and Smee reappeared. Rommy narrowed her eyes. Were her father's pockets lumpy, or was she imagining things?

Hook and Smee splashed back to the boat. Smee was carrying a long length of rough rope.

"You four boys and Finn, you're going to need to get out of the boat," said her father.

Jem and George shrunk back against Finn, and Walter tightened his arms around Finn's neck.

Her father let out a gusty breath. "What are you waiting for?" He swung an arm toward the sun which was no longer high over head. "We don't have time for theatrics."

Finn unlocked Walter's arms from around his neck and stood up. "What is it you want us to do, Captain?" he asked.

"Oh, the Capt'n has the best plan," said Smee, shifting from one foot to the other.

"Rommy was right earlier," said Hook. "We can't row up to my ship with all of you jammed into this boat like so many sardines. Nobody would believe you'd just come along so quietly." Hook rolled his eyes.

Finn lifted his chin. "So, how are we supposed to fool them?"

Hook smiled. "That is where you come in, my lad."

It only took a few minutes for her father to truss up Finn and the Lost Boys. Even though Rommy trusted her father, she still cringed when her father placed a rough loop of rope around Finn's neck and tied his hands behind his back. Smee then took the rope and tied each boys' hands to it so they were strung together in a long line.

By the time Smee had tied George's hands, Walter and Jem were both crying.

Finn twisted to look back at them. "It's all right, guys," he said. "This is all pretend."

Hook put a hand on Finn's shoulder. "Let them be," he said. "This lends just the right note of authenticity."

Finn shrugged her Hook's hand off his shoulder. "I don't care about no authen...whatever you said. I ain't just gonna let 'em be scared like that."

Hook shrugged his shoulders. "Do what you want," he said, "but if Corelli and some of the others sniff out what we're really up to, they'll have a real reason to be tafraid."

Chapter 29:
Fooling the Crew

The sun was much lower on the horizon when they finally rowed alongside her father's ship, Finn and the four Lost Boys flying behind them like a macabre kite.

It didn't take long before Rommy, Alice, Francie, and Tiger Lily were standing on the deck with her father.

Smee held the rope connected to the boys, and he gave it a rather vicious tug, pulling them all toward the deck. They landed awkwardly and Finn stumbled, only righting himself at the last minute. Rommy could hardly watch. The boys all looked so tired. She kept reminding herself this was all just part of the plan.

Hook strode to the bow of the boat and turned to address his crew. "There's more than one way to defeat our enemy," he said. He gestured to the boys who stood in a drooping row. "We'll deliver them to the workhouse. Poor Pan will be beside himself." A smile curved on his face, and he chuckled. "Now then, we will be pulling anchor before dawn. I want to be in the air before sunrise." He looked around at his men. "I need a volunteer to take a message to Pan. We wouldn't want him to worry over where his little friends went, now would we?"

Hook's eyes landed on Gentleman Jack. Rommy knew this was part of the plan. The message was just a ruse so that one of them could spy on Pan and the remaining Lost Boys.

"I would be happy to do that for you, Captain," said Gentleman Jack, giving a courtly bow in the direction of Hook.

Rommy watched the crew members, trying to read their expressions. Corelli, not surprisingly, had a sneer on his face. Smee was standing in the back, frowning.

Stubbs scratched his head. "Why don't we just make 'em walk the plank and be done with it, Cap'n?"

Hook whirled in the older man's direction and lifted one eyebrow. He lifted his hook to eye level, examined it, and said, "I hope you are not questioning your captain, Stubbs."

The older man gulped. "No...no...I...that is...I's just thought..." he stuttered.

Hook moved as fast as a snake and was in the older man's face. "I don't have you here to think, Stubbs, now do I?" he bellowed in the man's face.

The man leaned back and shook his head. "No, Cap'n, of course not, I..."

Hook leaned away and straightened his cuffs. He looked at the other men. "Does anyone else have any questions?" The silence stretched out for a long moment. "I thought not. You are dismissed to your duties." Hook gave a sharp nod, and the men began moving in various directions to fulfill their jobs.

Corelli moved closer to her father.

"What 'appened to you? Ya ain't injured are ya?" he asked gesturing at Hook's torn and bloody shirt.

Hook shrugged his big shoulders. "We had a little run-in with Pan, but no worries, I'm in perfect health, Corelli." Hook flashed a smile that was mostly teeth.

Corelli narrowed his eyes. "And what about the Indian wench?" he asked, nodding at Tiger Lily who stood rigidly next to Rommy.

Hook raised an eyebrow. "What about her?" he asked.

Corelli used his knife to pick something out of his teeth. "Ain't she a pal of Pan's? What's she doing here, roamin' around?"

Hook drew himself up and stared down his nose at the shorter man. "She is coming to England to join my daughter at school," he said.

"Since when is they such chums?" Corelli frowned at Tiger Lily and Rommy.

Hook's eyes narrowed. "My daughter and her friendships are none of your business," he snapped. "Instead of worrying about things that don't concern you, I suggest you get to work. We'll be pulling up anchor before the night is over."

Without waiting to see if Corelli had listened, Hook started giving orders to Smee.

The small, round man was at his side instantly.

"Take these boys down to the brig," he said. "Make sure they have food and water. We wouldn't want them to be too weak to work."

"Yes, sir, I'll take care of that right away," said Smee. He bustled over to Finn who stood at the front of the line. "You heard what the Captain said. Let's move along, and no funny business."

The boys shuffled forward, and Finn's eyes met Rommy's over the top of Smee's head. He gave her a small smile. Then without a word, he followed Smee.

Rommy walked over to where her father stood, a smile on his face as he watched his men moving about their tasks. He put a hand on her shoulder. "I think that went well, don't you, my dear?"

"I hope so," said Rommy. Unease slithered up her spine. From across the deck she could see Corelli, his eyes flicking to her father, a look of utter hatred on his face. Whether he believed Papa or not, they couldn't trust him. She squeezed her father's hand. "You need to watch your back around that man," she said.

"Don't worry, my dear, he won't get the jump on me," said Hook. "I've been around men like him before."

Rommy nodded, but she kept her eyes on the burly man. She wanted to believe this plan would work, but there was a sinking feeling in her stomach that was hard to ignore.

Chapter 30:
Deception in Motion

Rommy, Alice, and Francie sat on the bed in Rommy's cabin. Tiger Lily leaned against one of the walls. Rommy wasn't sure what time it was, but it had to be nearing dawn in a few hours. Even though everyone must have been as exhausted as she felt, nobody wanted to miss anything. In only a few more hours, they would be leaving Neverland forever.

With her father.

If things went as planned.

Tiger Lily straightened and began pacing back and forth.

"Can't you sit down?" asked Francie. "You're making even me nervous."

"Something does not feel right," said Tiger Lily.

Rommy couldn't deny that the same feeling had been nagging her most of the evening. In fact, she had barely eaten any dinner.

"What does that even mean?" said Francie and blew out a breath. "We only have a few more hours before we can leave, right? We just have to sit tight until then."

Rommy shook her head. "Tiger Lily's right," she said. "It just seems too easy." She paused and then said, "I don't like that

Finn and the others are tied up below decks. And where are the fairies? And Tinkerbell?"

Tiger Lily shook her head. "The fairies would not want to be anywhere near your father," she said. Seeing Rommy's face, she lifted a shoulder. "Enchanting this ship came at a great cost."

"And Tink's probably back in that tree in the middle of the swamp," said Alice.

Rommy felt disappointment spear through her. She looked down at her hands. She had hoped to see Nissa and the rest at least one more time. At least to thank them for all they had done. She had expected them to see the quest through to the end, but then, maybe they saw the end of the quest as turning the key.

"You're probably right about the fairies," she said. "I had forgotten their bad history with Papa."

"Does yer old man have a good history with anyone?" Alice asked.

Rommy felt her cheeks heat. "I suppose you're right," she said, her voice small.

Alice patted her arm. "It ain't yer fault," she said. "'Sides, maybe leaving this place will do him good."

Rommy put her arm around Alice and hugged her. "I hope so," she said.

Francie's head started to nod, and she jerked back upright. Rommy patted her shoulder. "If you're that tired, Francie, why don't you sleep a bit? There's still an hour or two to sunrise, I think."

Francie nodded drowsily and without further encouragement, she curled up on her side. Alice flopped down next to her and yawned hugely.

"Ain't you sleepy?" she asked Rommy.

Rommy shook her head. She didn't want to say she couldn't shake the uneasiness that had been plaguing her for the last several hours. Rommy opened her mouth to speak only to realize that both Francie and Alice had already dozed off.

Tiger Lily stopped pacing and looked down at the sleeping girls. "I cannot sleep, either," she said. "I will scout things out." She turned toward the door.

Rommy hopped to her feet and put a hand on the other girl's arm. "I don't know if that's a good idea," she said. "You may arouse suspicion, and besides, I don't know how safe it is. Maybe I should go instead."

Tiger Lily raised an eyebrow. "Nobody will know I am about," she said and then sniffed. "The same cannot be said of you."

"It's not safe for you," Rommy said again. "I'm the captain's daughter. All the men know my father will keelhaul them if they bother with me." She crossed her arms. "The same cannot be said for you."

Tiger Lily pursed her lips and then let out a breath. "You probably speak the truth," she said. "Come, we will go together." She walked purposefully toward the door.

Rommy got there first and put her hand on the knob. "Let me at least see who's out there first."

Tiger Lily merely shrugged. Rommy slowly opened the door. She had a moment of déjà vu from when she and Alice had sneaked off the ship what seemed like ages ago. Tiger Lily poked her in the back.

"Why are you not moving?" the other girl asked.

"Just a minute," said Rommy "I want to make sure there isn't anyone about. It's awfully late, and I don't want to make anyone suspicious."

She peered around the door and down the narrow path beside the cabin. The light from the lanterns on the main deck cast shadows back here.

"Where do they keep the boys?" Tiger Lily asked.

"I'm not sure," said Rommy.

"We must look," said Tiger Lily.

"We can't just wander around looking for the brig," said Rommy.

"Why not?" asked Tiger Lily.

"Well, because...won't the men wonder why we're doing that?"

"You worry too much," said Tiger Lily. "As you say, the men know you are the Captain's daughter." She drew herself up. "I am the Chief's daughter. My people do not question why I am here or there."

Rommy paused. Maybe Tiger Lily had a point. Maybe skulking around would be more suspicious than just taking a little walk.

"Perhaps you're right," she said. "I can just say we were curious about what getting the ship ready to leave looks like."

Tiger Lily smiled in approval. The two girls stepped out into the space that ran along the cabin walls and walked toward the main deck, which bustled with activity despite the late hour.

Chapter 31:
Fool Me Once

The two girls dodged around the men and made their way to the bow of the boat where they both leaned against the railing. Tiger Lily had been right. Nobody questioned what they were doing out of their cabin.

Rommy looked out over the water. The moon's light sent fingers of silver over the gentle waves of the Cove where the ship bobbed. After a moment, she turned back to look at the deck. Lanterns cast a warm glow over the men as they worked.

Rommy's eyes roved from group to group. Big Red stood with his arms crossed, barking orders at several of the men, including Stubbs, who was complaining rather loudly about why they were all still up. Corelli was there, too, his bald head bent toward his task, but he kept looking around furtively.

A trickle of unease made her stomach queasy. She didn't see Gentleman Jack anywhere. She looked around for her father. Maybe the two men were together somewhere else on the ship.

Just then the door to Hook's cabin swung open, and he strode out onto the deck, Smee rushing along in his wake. He spotted Rommy and made his way over, Smee trailing behind him.

When he reached the two of them, he frowned. "You girls should be back in your cabin. It's late," he said.

Rommy shook her head. "I can't sleep, and besides, I've never seen what all it takes to get the ship ready to go."

Hook opened his mouth, but Smee interrupted him. "Aw, Capt'n, what'll it hurt to let the girl and her friend watch for a little while. We have a long trip back to London. They can get their beauty rest then."

Her father looked like he wanted to argue, but then he shrugged. "All right, but stay up here, out of the way," he said. "I don't want either of you to get hurt." He gave Rommy a meaningful glance.

She reached up to hug him and took that opportunity to whisper in his ear. "Where's Gentleman Jack? Shouldn't he be back by now?"

"Don't you worry. He knows what he's about," Papa said quietly before releasing her and straightening.

Rommy opened her mouth to protest, but he held up his hand. "Let it be, my dear," he said. "You've done your job; now let me do mine."

He turned to the men and held up his hands for their attention. The clattering on the deck gradually became silent as the men waited for what their captain had to say.

Hook smiled benevolently at them all. "Perhaps I am becoming kinder in my old age," he looked down at Rommy. "Or perhaps it is having my daughter onboard, but I have decided to give you a choice about our next excursion."

A murmur moved through the crowd of men. Apparently, Captain Hook did not give choices very often.

"Our trip to London will be longer than normal. I have several tasks that I need to complete while we are there," he let a thin smile curl across his face, "besides delivering our little present." There was a ripple of laughter from the men. "I also want to spend some time with my daughter and get her friend settled into the academy. This means we will be gone for at least a month."

Rommy heard the undercurrent of talking amongst the men. Her father held up his hands again, and once again silence descended.

"I know some of you aren't too keen to spend too much time within England's welcoming embrace," he smirked, "so you may choose to stay here. You will need to let me know as soon as possible, and I will only allow the first 10 to stay." Her father chuckled. "After all, I need someone to man my ship."

The group of men erupted in conversation, and several shoved their way toward Hook. He squeezed her shoulder and gave her a little push toward her friend, out of the way of the pirates now crowding around him.

Rommy made her way to Tiger Lily. "Where do you think we should look for that door to the brig?"

The words had barely left her mouth when Smee came bustling up to them. "There you are, my darling girl," he said, stopping in front of her.

She smiled at the small, round man. "Hello, Smee," she said. "Does Papa need me?"

He shook his head. "Oh no, my dear," he said. He looked around and then leaned toward her. "Your young man wants a word." He winked at her.

Tiger Lily choked back a snort, and Rommy felt her cheeks heat up. "I'm not sure what you mean, Mr. Smee. I don't have a young man," she said.

He patted her cheek. "Now, now, Miss, let's not be coy," he said. "We'll just nip down, and you have a word with Finn, and nobody will be the wiser."

A flash of panic welled up in Rommy. "Is something wrong?" she asked.

Smee seemed flustered for a moment. "Oh no," he said, "nothing like that. Not at all."

Relief flooded over Rommy. "Okay," she said. She stood and gestured to Tiger Lily, but Smee stepped between them. He put his mouth near her ear. "I think your young man would like a private word."

Rommy flushed. "Well, I guess," she said. She turned to the other girl who raised her eyebrows. Rommy put her hand briefly at her waist where her dagger was strapped. "I won't be long. Maybe you can meet me back at the cabin."

Tiger Lily merely nodded.

Smee bustled ahead of her, and she followed him, skirting the men who were still clumped around her father.

Smee led her toward the cabins and then around the side toward the back of the boat, which got more shadowy the farther they went.

They cleared the side of the cabins, but a commotion on the main deck caused Rommy to twist back around. Smee grabbed her hand and pulled her forward.

"Just a little further, my dear," he said.

Rommy stumbled and put a hand on the railing to right herself. She looked around and frowned. "I didn't know the door to the brig was back here," she said. She looked around but didn't see anything that could be a door. She looked back at Smee in confusion.

He had backed up several steps and there was a sad smile on his face. "I'm so sorry, my dear," he said.

Confusion and a growing sense of alarm made her swing back toward the sounds from the main deck. But before she could take a single step, a bag came over her head and blocked her vision. Someone put an arm around her neck and pulled her roughly back. A horribly familiar voice spoke in her ear.

"You're mine now," said Peter Pan. "Now and forever."

Chapter 32:

Everyone Has an Agenda

Rommy felt her breath go out in a whoosh, and a cold ball formed in her stomach. The inside of the bag smelled like sweaty feet, and she gagged a little.

She shook her head, trying to clear her thoughts. It took a moment for Smee's treachery to register in her brain. She twisted her head in the direction he'd been standing. "Why, Mr. Smee?" she asked.

Smee's voice was muffled. "I can't let the Captain leave Neverland," he said. She heard the man tsk several times. "As usual, he just doesn't know what's good for him. I have to take care of him, my dear." She felt him pat her hand. "And we know he won't leave without his darling daughter. Now don't you worry your pretty little head. It'll all work out. You'll see." She heard him turn away and start walking.

Pan laughed in her ear. She shivered and tried to slow her breathing. Calm. She had to stay calm. She didn't know what time it was, but it had to be only an hour or two, maybe less, to dawn.

"Come along now," Smee said. "We need her on the main deck."

Pan pushed her forward, and she stumbled. His arm came around her waist and pulled her closer. She tried to pull away.

"It's okay, Rommy," he said. "I won't let those pirates hurt you. You'll see. We'll be happy here. Together."

Rommy stayed silent and tried to listen to her surroundings. He moved her forward again, and she shuffled her feet, afraid of tripping. As they made their way back toward the main deck, the sounds of swords clashing and fighting got louder and louder.

Pan stopped, and the lights of the deck penetrated the cloth over her face. Smee gave a loud, shrill whistle and the sounds on the deck died down.

She heard her father bellow, "Smee, what is the meaning of this?"

"Now, Captain, you need to settle down," said Smee. "This is all for your own good."

"Pan, unhand my daughter at once, or you will regret it with every fiber of your being." Her father's voice was loud and commanding.

Rommy heard a harsh laugh and guessed it was Corelli. "I don't think you get it, Captain," said the rough voice. "You ain't givin' the orders anymore." There was a pause, and then Rommy felt something cold and sharp press against her neck. She froze.

"Nah-ah, Captain," the pirate said. "Unless you'd like to see your pretty little girl's throat slit, I suggest you drop that sword."

"No," Rommy yelled, her hands clutching into nothing. "No, don't do it, Papa."

Pan pulled her in tighter. "Don't fight," he said. "I don't mind making you bleed a little." Rommy tried to twist away from him, but she felt the cold blade bite into her neck. She stilled.

A guttural laugh sounded. "Brave little thing, I'll say that for her," said the voice. "Aww, Captain," the word was said with a sneer, "don't look like that now. As long as you do what I say, I won't harm your daughter. I just want this ship. I don't care a tuppence about her. She can go play with the Lost Boys for all I care." The man's voice got harder. "Or she can join you at the bottom of the sea. The choice is yours. Now drop your sword."

A metallic clatter made Rommy's heart sink to her toes. Her mind flew from her father to the girls to the Lost Boys to Finn.

A loud cry startled Rommy so much she jerked, and Pan's knife bit deeper into her throat. A warm wetness trickled down her neck.

"You liar," cried Smee.

The guttural laugh sounded again. "You stupid old man," he said. "Did you really think I was going to turn the ship back to the Captain here?"

There was a pause and then a terrible scream followed by a dull thump.

She heard Smee's voice, garbled now. "I'm sorry, Cap'n. I only...wanted...to...save..." And then a horrible gurgling sound before everything became silent.

Rommy squeezed her eyes shut even though she couldn't see anything. Poor Smee.

Corelli's voice rang over the deck once more. "Nobody else has to die—well, except for the dear old Captain here, as we can't have him running around loose. Swear allegiance to me, and you can live."

There was the sound of scuffling, and then Corelli spoke again. "There's always a few in every crew." He made a disgusted sound. "Dumb blokes! All right, round them up with the Captain."

Pan started to float upwards, taking Rommy with him. She kicked against him. There was no way she was leaving her father, not now.

"Shh," Pan hissed in her ear.

"Stop right there, Pan," said Corelli.

"You promised I could have her," said Pan. "You have the Captain. You don't need her anymore." Pan floated higher.

"Go any further and I'll shoot her and then you," said Corelli. Pan drifted to a halt. Corelli continued, "The good Captain still has a few secrets we don't want him takin' to his grave with him. And he won't be nearly as agreeable if his daughter isn't right here to convince him, isn't that right?"

Rommy heard the muffled sound of something hard hitting flesh. She flinched again, and tears welled up in her eyes. She blinked them away. Now wasn't the time to start crying. Think, she told herself. There had to be a way out of this.

"That pride of yours needs to go," said Corelli. Another thump and a faint groan made Rommy bite her lip.

"Bring her here," said Corelli.

Pan didn't move.

A loud blast made Rommy's ears ring, and something whistled by her ear.

"I said, bring her here, Pan," said Corelli. "The next shot will go right through that lovely forehead."

Pan hissed but flew downward. They landed on the deck, and the bag was whipped from her head. Rommy blinked against the lamplight, trying to adjust her sight.

Her father was standing in front of Corelli, his hands bound behind his back. Blood trickled from the corner of his mouth, but that didn't stop the sneer from twisting his face.

Corelli reached out and grabbed her by the hair and jerked her toward him. She stumbled away from Pan, but the boy's dirk snaked out and was pointed at Corelli's throat before she could right herself.

"Let go," said Pan. "You have the Captain. I won't let you hurt what is mine to play your stupid games. Do that on your own time."

Corelli snarled at Pan and pointed his revolver at the boy, but Pan's dirk did not waver from Corelli's neck.

"Do you think you can pull that trigger before I can slice your neck?" Pan asked conversationally.

Corelli didn't let go of Rommy's hair.

"I can't control him without his daughter," said Corelli. "We had a deal."

Her father snorted. "Good luck with getting Peter Pan to honor that."

"Shut up," said Corelli and swung the revolver toward her father.

So fast that his movements were a blur, Pan sliced the hand tangled in Rommy's hair and tried to pull her away from the pirate. But Corelli's grip didn't loosen. Rommy yelped as Pan pulled one way, and Corelli kept a viciously tight grip on her hair. She felt like a bone between two rabid dogs.

Blood dripped down Corelli's arm but he didn't loosen his hold. "Keep it up, boy, and I'll snap her neck." He gave another savage yank, and Rommy bit her lip to keep from crying out as her neck wrenched at a painful angle.

"I won't let you take what's mine," said Pan, his eyes narrowing.

"Let go and back up," Corelli said, waving his revolver at the boy.

Pan paused, and Corelli moved the gun until it was pointed at Rommy.

Pan smiled. "If you shoot her, what's making the Captain here do what you want?"

Her father chuckled. "The boy does have a point, Corelli."

Corelli snarled in her father's direction, but he had learned his lesson. The gun stayed trained on Rommy.

"If I can't use her to make him cooperate, she's useless to me anyway," said Corelli. He cocked the gun and smiled so widely his gold tooth winked in the lamp light. "Say goodbye."

Pan scowled but abruptly let go of Rommy. Corelli jerked her toward him and put a beefy arm round her throat. He stuck the gun in his waistband.

"Now then," he said looking at Hook, "what's say you and I have a heart to heart, eh, Captain?"

Her father looked down his nose at the other man, his eyes cold. "The only heart you'll see is your own when I rip it, still beating, out of your chest."

"Now, now, Captain," chided the other man, "is that any way to talk?"

Without warning, he backhanded her father across the face. Hook's head snapped back from the impact, but he merely shook his head, working his jaw from side to side. One eyebrow rose as if Corelli was a mere annoyance.

Rommy's eyes went to her father's face, and for just a moment, as their eyes met, she saw anguish there. Then the cold mask of fury slammed back down.

"As I was saying," the pirate said. He leaned forward, and his dirty fingers dipped into the front pocket of Hook's leather coat. When they reappeared, a ruby the size of a robin's egg was pinched between his fingers. "Why don't you tell me where I can find the rest of these jewels, and I'll let your little girl here go."

"Your word isn't worth considering," said Hook.

"Maybe, maybe not," said Corelli, tucking the jewel into his own pocket, "but I can tell you, if you don't tell me where to find these jewels, you won't be the only one to feed the fishes, and that's a promise I aim to keep." He tightened his arm around Rommy's throat, making her breathing difficult.

Her father kept his eyes trained on Corelli. "That's a dangerous promise to make," he said.

Corelli shook his head. "Still making threats, I see," he said. "Let's see if you keep that so proper stiff English upper lip when other people suffer for your stubbornness."

He turned and pointed at Tommy. "Sorry, lad, but you had your chance to join me."

Tommy glowered at him. "I wouldn't join you if you was the last pirate around."

Corelli grinned, his gold tooth flashing in the lamplight. "Well, I'll be the last pirate you see, boyo." He nodded at Stubbs who was holding Tommy. The old man blanched.

"But...but...sir," said Stubbs.

Corelli didn't say a word. He simply pulled the gun from his waistband and fired. The old pirate hit the deck with a thud. Rommy turned her eyes from the still form.

The silence that fell on the deck was deafening.

"That's one down, so many more to go," said Corelli. He moved the gun to track Tommy's movements. The boy had crouched down when the gun had gone off and was scuttling toward the rail of the ship. The other pirates were still too stunned to move.

Rommy knew she had to distract Corelli before he shot Tommy. She only hoped the man wouldn't kill her for it.

She squinted in the lamplight and made out Big Red and Max, who also had their hands bound behind their backs. She didn't see Gentleman Jack anywhere and hoped he would make it back in time to help them.

Suddenly, from the corner of her eye, a light caught her attention. Moving her head ever so slightly, she saw several tiny glowing orbs came into view. She blinked, not sure if she was seeing things because of lack of oxygen, but no, Nissa, Balo, Kalen, and Talen were here. Hope sprang up in her chest. Now all she had to do was stall Corelli.

Before she could second-guess herself, Rommy let her eyes flutter shut. She went limp.

Chapter 33:
Pride Goes Before the Fall

The sudden shift of Rommy's body weight, slight though it was, threw Corelli off balance. He stumbled slightly. A blast ripped through the night. Rommy kept her eyes shut and her body limp, but she could hear the commotion as men dove for cover. Corelli's arm tightened around her neck, and she wondered if she really would pass out from lack of air.

Just when she thought she was going under, he jostled her around so she was tucked under his arm like a bundle of sticks.

"Blast females!" Corelli said.

She felt him turn in a partial circle. "Get out from there, ya bunch of cowards," he said, his voice rising. "Or the next shot will find its mark."

The pirate's arm was like a vice around her waist, and she hung at an uncomfortable angle. At least she was making things more difficult for him, so she kept her eyes shut and willed her body to stay loose.

He grunted and hefted her up again. It was all Rommy could do to keep up the ruse of being unconscious.

"Now then, Captain, who d'you like to see get it next?" asked Corelli. He seemed to have gotten his composure back.

Rommy only hoped Tommy had been able to slip away in all the confusion.

She slitted her eyes open. She was hanging over the pirate's arm so that her head was upside down, but she still had a partial view.

Suddenly, blasts of light lit up the deck.

Rommy took the opportunity presented and reared up, smashing the back of her head into Corelli's face. She heard a satisfying crunch. The man roared with pain and dropped her onto the deck. She landed hard on her side, momentarily stunned. She shook her head and rolled toward the railing. Another blast from Corelli's gun deafened her, and she felt something hot skim by her ear and land with a thwack into the wood just behind her. She scrabbled to her feet, dodging toward one of the masts.

Looking back over her shoulder, she saw her father rear back and head-butt Corelli in his already-broken nose, making the man stagger back. Taking advantage of his being off-balance, her father kicked the man in the chest, sending him crashing to the deck, the gun spinning out of his hand.

Rommy backed up to the rail, looking around wildly for any kind of weapon. Suddenly, a figure hurtled down from the rigging, sending the two pirates guarding Big Red and Max crashing to the deck. It took only a moment for Gentleman Jack to free his fellow pirates.

Her father was battling with Corelli, and Big Red, Max, and Gentleman Jack were fighting the other pirates. Rommy reached for her dagger, but just as her fingers touched the hilt, an arm snaked around her and yanked her backwards.

She tossed her head backwards, trying to hit whoever held her, but the high-pitched laugh sent an icy chill over her skin. She had forgotten about Pan.

"Clever girl," Pan said, "but I've already seen you do that trick."

Rommy struggled to get away from him, but his hold tightened. She felt his blade against her throat again.

"Stop it," he said, jerking her even closer until she could barely breathe. This was getting so old. "Don't you want to see who wins?"

Rommy stilled and looked down. From up here, she could see the entire deck spread out below. She watched as Finn dodged between pirates and swords until he had reached her father, who was fighting Corelli even though his arms were still bound behind him. Finn slid behind him, and suddenly Papa was free.

Her father pulled out the sword still strapped to his waist. With a guttural bellow he charged into the fray, slashing and swiping.

Rommy stared as her father whirled through the pirates like a dancer of death. Corelli had scrambled for his gun and was pointing it at her father.

Rommy opened her mouth to scream, but her father was already there, his sword neatly sliding into Corelli. The man's mouth opened in surprise, and he stood there staring for a moment before he slumped to his knees. Then he slowly fell to his side, his eyes still open in shock.

"I do so admire the Captain and his fighting skills," said Pan. He shook his head and let out a tsk. "Corelli was not very smart to leave your father with his sword. It looks like that mistake cost him."

Rommy stared down at her father, who stood in the middle of the deck, his black hair flowing behind him. He had his sword in one hand, and his hook gleamed in the lamplight. All the pirates that had turned on him were now on their knees, their hands behind their heads.

Pan started to pull her backwards. "Time for us to go," he said.

Rommy snapped back to the present.

"No," she said, twisting and kicking against Pan. "I don't belong here."

"I keep telling you, you're wrong. You do belong—with me," said Pan, dragging her backward, away from the ship. "You'll see."

The stars above her were starting to wink out. The moon had slid down behind the clouds, and Rommy knew her time was running out.

The deck receded from below her feet, and she dimly heard her father calling her name. She refused to be stuck here forever. Pan wasn't going to win this one. Not now, not after all that she had gone through.

Straining forward, she bit his wrist. He screeched and his hold loosened. She wrenched away, darting back toward the ship.

He grabbed her ankle, halting her progress. She grabbed her dagger and twisted back, slashing at him. He yelped and let go.

Again, she rocketed toward the ship. Again, he grabbed her, this time by the back of her shirt. She reached behind her and hacked at his arm, and the drag holding her disappeared. Down she went again, but he tackled her midair, sending them both tumbling.

She twisted and bucked, and her foot connected solidly with his middle. He shrieked and let go of her, bending double.

Rommy flew toward the deck again, Pan's screams following her downward. Her heart thundered in her ears. She was almost there. Suddenly, a searing pain ripped through her scalp. She jerked to a halt, the pain making her eyes tear up. She tried to pull away, but the ripping at her scalp made spots dance in front of her eyes. Suddenly she stopped fighting Pan and let him pull her close.

Pan was caught off-balance, allowing her to swivel around in his grip. She smacked her head against the bridge of his nose, and his grip fell away from her hair. She shoved with both hands, sending him backwards.

She landed on the ship, gasping for breath. Her father ran toward her, only steps away, but Pan flew between them. He smashed the hilt of his dirk into Hook's nose and blood spurted in a red arc. Pan wrapped an arm around Rommy's waist, but someone tackled him from the side, sending them both spinning off the boat into the air. Rommy was flung to the deck, the breath knocked from her lungs.

Her father knelt next to her as she gasped for air. "Go," she wheezed. "We have to leave." She pointed a shaking finger toward the horizon where the faintest of glows was just visible.

Her father jumped to his feet. "Jack, get those men down to the brig," he shouted. "The rest of you, weigh anchor and hoist the mizzen."

Rommy pushed herself to a sitting position as the ship beneath her creaked. Within a moment, it began to glow with pixie dust as it surged forward and began to lift off the surface of the water.

In the sky Finn and Pan grappled with each other. Rommy lurched to her feet, her eyes trained on the two boys above her head. She bunched her legs beneath her, but her father caught her around the waist. He pulled her into his broad chest.

"No, Rommy, you can't," he said. "There's no time left." She knew he was right. The glow in the horizon was getting brighter. The ship lifted with a creak into the sky.

"No," she cried, "we can't leave him. Finn!"

There was a pause as the two boys separated for a moment. Across the space, Rommy's hazel eyes met Finn's gray ones. He grinned at her and winked. Then he dove back at Pan.

Tears blurred Rommy's vision so that she barely saw the dark gray streak. Her father's arms were like bands of iron keeping her rooted to the deck. She stopped struggling and sagged back against him.

It was too late.

The ship picked up speed and burst forward with a loud sucking sound. Neverland became smaller and blurry until it disappeared from view, and all that she could see were the gold and pink clouds of sunrise.

She turned in her father's arms, buried her face in his chest, and sobbed.

Chapter 34:
This is Happily Ever After?

Rommy heard her father murmuring and felt his cheek against her hair. Alice and Francie crowded close, and she could feel hands patting her and hear soothing words. But a horrible ache had taken up residence in her chest, and she didn't know if it would ever go away.

Finn. Finn had saved her, and now he was gone. Forever. The thought brought a fresh torrent of tears.

"I'm so sorry, my dear," Hook murmured.

She wasn't sure how long she'd been crying when she heard someone clearing their throat. Francie was pulling on her sleeve.

"Rommy? Rommy?"

Rommy lifted her head from her father's chest and blinked her red, swollen eyes. She heard Alice giggle and felt a spurt of annoyance.

"I think you'd best wipe your eyes, darling," said her father and when she looked up, he was smiling.

What was wrong with everyone? Didn't they realize Finn was gone?

She turned to say as much to her friends, and that was when she saw Finn perched on the rail of the ship. The next thing she knew, Finn was pulling himself over the edge, Balo and Nissa next to him.

Rommy's eyes widened. "Finn? But how...I thought..."

He pushed his hair out of his eyes and grinned at her. "It was Tinkerbell," he said. "She come zooming in and started firing those magic balls of fire at Pan. He was yelpin' and trying to get away. You didn't have to tell me twice to get going."

He took a step toward her, his smile softening as he gestured toward her red eyes. "Don't tell me all that was for me."

She ran across the deck and threw her arms around him. "You big daft idiot, of course it was for you," she said and squeezed him a bit tighter as his arms came around her. "Oh, Finn, I thought you were gone forever." Her voice caught. "Because of me."

"Aw, don't start crying again," he said, patting her back awkwardly.

She pulled back and punched him in the arm.

"Hey," he said, rubbing his arm, but he was still smiling. "Is that any way to treat the hero of the day?"

"Hero?" she spluttered.

"Yeah, hero," he said.

And putting both hands on either side of her face, he leaned forward and kissed her. Her eyes fluttered shut, and she leaned into him. Everyone else faded into the background, and it was just her and Finn.

Then her father cleared his throat.

They jerked apart. Rommy's cheeks turned bright red, and Finn looked at Hook, panic washing over his face.

A smile ghosted across Hook's face. "I'm sure you're overcome with emotion, and I won't be seeing a repeat, isn't that right, young man?"

Finn swallowed. "Um, yes, sir. Of course, sir."

He glanced at Rommy, who smiled at him.

Then everyone was crowding around. Francie let out a whoop, and Alice clapped her hands. The Lost Boys hung on Finn's arms and legs. Even Tiger Lily was smiling.

Rommy looked up to see her father standing a little apart, a smile on his face. Following her gaze, Finn squeezed her hand and nodded. She disengaged from the rest of them and came to stand by Hook, leaning into him. His arm came around her shoulder.

Part of the crew was busy trimming sails and steering the ship, and several of the men were mopping dark smudges on the deck. She quickly looked away. Smee, Corelli, and Stubbs were nowhere to be seen, and Rommy pushed her last memory of them down deep.

"This has been quite the adventure," said her father.

Rommy sighed. "It's hard to believe I left Chattingham's not even two weeks ago," she said.

"I don't know that I could have survived if it had been much longer." He gave a wry smile and hugged her closer. "I think it's high time we went home, don't you?"

Rommy nodded. She couldn't agree with him more.

Epilogue
April 1911
Tottenham, England

Rommy sat in the small visiting parlor, waiting for her father. It was her 13th birthday. She couldn't believe it had been a year since that fateful day when her father had failed to show up.

Things had changed drastically since then. While her father still was in charge of a vast shipping enterprise, he ran it mostly from his offices on the London docks. This summer, they planned to take a trip to their estates in St. Croix. Francie was coming with her, and, of course, Tiger Lily and Alice would be with them, too, since her father had formally adopted both girls.

Finn had become her father's ward and apprentice. Papa had enrolled him in Chattingham's sister school for boys, the Worthington Young Men's Academy. However, since Finn did not take to formal education after years of running wild in Neverland. Her father, realizing Finn wasn't doing well and had hired a tutor to catch the boy up on the basics and then made Finn his apprentice. This, more than anything, proved to Rommy that her father had really changed.

Finn, for his part, had showed a surprisingly good head for business. While he was still too young at 15 to step into a main role in her father's enterprise, Finn had proven to be an apt pupil under her father's tutelage. He had also taken over a lot of the work Smee had once done as her father's clerk. Her father had even brought Finn up to several of her fencing matches and allowed them to correspond. Francie teased her unmercifully about him, but she didn't have much room to talk since she spent half her time mooning over Max.

The four young Lost Boys had been returned to their thankful families. It had been difficult explaining what had happened to the boys. In the end, her father had simply said the boys had been shanghaied by pirates, and he had found them on his travels. As fantastical as that sounded, it was far more believable than the truth.

It had also been a bit of a challenge to come up with a convincing story of why she had disappeared from the school grounds for so long. In the end, her father had donated the funds for a new astronomy observatory and agreed to forget that the school had misplaced his daughter for better than a week.

Miss Cleo, the resident cat, sauntered into the room and leaped into Rommy's lap. She put her face into the cat's soft fur and the animal purred.

The door creaked open, and her father walked into the room.

Putting the cat down, Rommy ran across the room and threw her arms around her father. He lifted her off her feet and whirled her in a circle.

"How's my girl?" he said.

He set her down and kissed her cheek.

"Papa, my tournament dueling match is next week," said Rommy, shifting from one foot to the other in her excitement. "Will you be able to come? Can you bring Finn, too?"

"Yes, Captain Cavendish," said a cool voice from the doorway. "We hope you and your ward will be able to join us." Miss Watson stood at the door with the tea tray.

James Cavendish gave a courtly bow in the teacher's direction and then walked over to take the tray from her. "Of course," he said. "I wouldn't miss it for the world."

Miss Watson smiled. "I know Rommy will be delighted for you to be there."

Her father winked at the teacher who turned pink. "No, ma'am, the delight is all mine."

Rommy looked from her father to her favorite teacher and suppressed a giggle.

"Miss Watson, you should join us for our tea," she said. "You can tell Papa about our writing club."

"Oh, I wouldn't want to interrupt, Rommy," her teacher protested. "This is your time with your father."

"It's all right," said Rommy and looked at her father.

He cleared his throat. "We'd love to have you join us, Miss Watson, and do tell about this writing club."

Miss Watson perched on the edge of one of the chairs. She placed a small powdered lemon confection on a plate. "Well, we started a writing club this year, and Rommy is our star pupil." She gave Rommy a brilliant smile. "She has quite the imagination, what with her stories about pirates and fairies and such. She's come up with some quite fantastical ideas."

Rommy and her father exchanged glances. She suppressed a grin and looked down at her teacup, and her father coughed into his hand. Then he focused back on her teacher. "You don't say?"

The two hours passed in a happy blur. Finally, Miss Watson stood up. "Oh dear, I do apologize for taking all of your time," she said. She looked at Rommy. "I'm afraid it's almost time to get ready for bed. Why don't I leave you to say your goodbyes?"

Her father stood and bowed over Miss Watson's hand, kissing her knuckles. The teacher blushed to the roots of her hair but managed to leave the room with her dignity still intact. Rommy noticed her father watched Miss Watson all the way out of the room and hid her smile.

Papa turned to her and drew her into a hug. She squeezed him back and walked with him toward the door.

"So, you'll be able to make it next Saturday?" she asked again when they reached the doorway to the parlor.

"I wouldn't miss it," he said.

Dropping a kiss on the top of her head, he turned to leave. "I'll see you soon, my dear."

Rommy hugged the words to her and waved until Papa disappeared from sight. She and her father were finally home.

Afterward

Thanks for picking up *Neverland's Key!* I hope you enjoyed it. If you have a minute, **I'd love it if you'd leave an honest review** on your online retailer of choice or Goodreads. This helps other people find the book, too.

If you'd like to keep up with my new releases, favorite book deals, and fun giveaways, be sure to sign up for my monthly newsletter. As a thank you, you will receive a free digital bookclub toolkit. You can sign up at http://www.rvbowman.com/u4fz.

If you want to check out the other books in the **Pirate Princess Chronicles**, you can get *Hook's Daughter* and *Pan's Secret* at all major online book retailers.

Don't miss out!

Visit the website below and you can sign up to receive emails whenever R.V. Bowman publishes a new book. There's no charge and no obligation.

https://books2read.com/r/B-A-JZDH-CICCB

BOOKS 2 READ

Connecting independent readers to independent writers.

About the Author

R.V. Bowman spends her days wrangling middle-school students while secretly trying to instill a love of language without any of them realizing it. By night, she writes fantastical adventures full of magic and heart.

Her love of books began as a child when she would pester anyone within earshot to read her a story. Once she learned to read on her own, her grandmother fed her reading addiction with a steady supply of books. R.V. Bowman lives in Northwest Ohio with her husband, two sons, and a very hairy dog named Kipper.

Read more at www.rvbowman.com.